# LOVE HATE IRRELEVANCE

L. C. PAOLETTI

## Copyright

Love Hate Irrelevance by Lawrence C. Paoletti
Copyright © 2019 L. C. Paoletti

**All Rights Reserved**

This material may not be republished, rewritten or redistributed without the express written consent of the publisher except for use of brief quotations in a book review.
Printed in the United States of America.
First Printing, 2019
ISBN 978-0-9975617-4-6 Paperback Edition
ISBN 978-0-9975617-5-3 E-Book Edition
L.C. Paoletti, Publisher
www.lcpaoletti.com

**Disclaimer**

This novel is an original work of fiction. The resemblance of any character in this novel to you or to anyone you know resides solely in your imagination, and while the name of some businesses, locations and institutions are real they are used in a strictly fictional manner.

**Cover Design and Artwork**

The cover was designed by Sabine Delizia Egger using three of her original acrylic paintings. Sabine is an artist who lives and creates in Österreich, Austria. The full color version of each painting is shown after each story title on color-supported ebook readers. Learn more about Sabine and her art at: https://www.delizia.at

## CONTENTS

1. LOVE ............................................. 1
   Page 49 .......................................... 4
   Cross ............................................ 5
   Me .............................................. 10
   Friday .......................................... 13
   Weekend ......................................... 17
   Melrose-Cedar Park .............................. 19
   Expressions ..................................... 25
   Empty Soul ...................................... 31
   Gone ............................................ 32
   Love's Author ................................... 35
   Epilogue ........................................ 39
2. HATE ........................................... 41
   Word ............................................ 44
   Logic ........................................... 45
   Ghosts .......................................... 47
   Aghast .......................................... 49
   Guilty .......................................... 51
   Unwanted seed ................................... 53
   Cell X .......................................... 58
   Appeal .......................................... 85
   Epilogue ........................................ 86
3. IRRELEVANCE .................................... 89
   Room K78 ........................................ 92

   *ACKNOWLEDGEMENT* ............................. 123
   *About the Author* ............................ 125

# LOVE

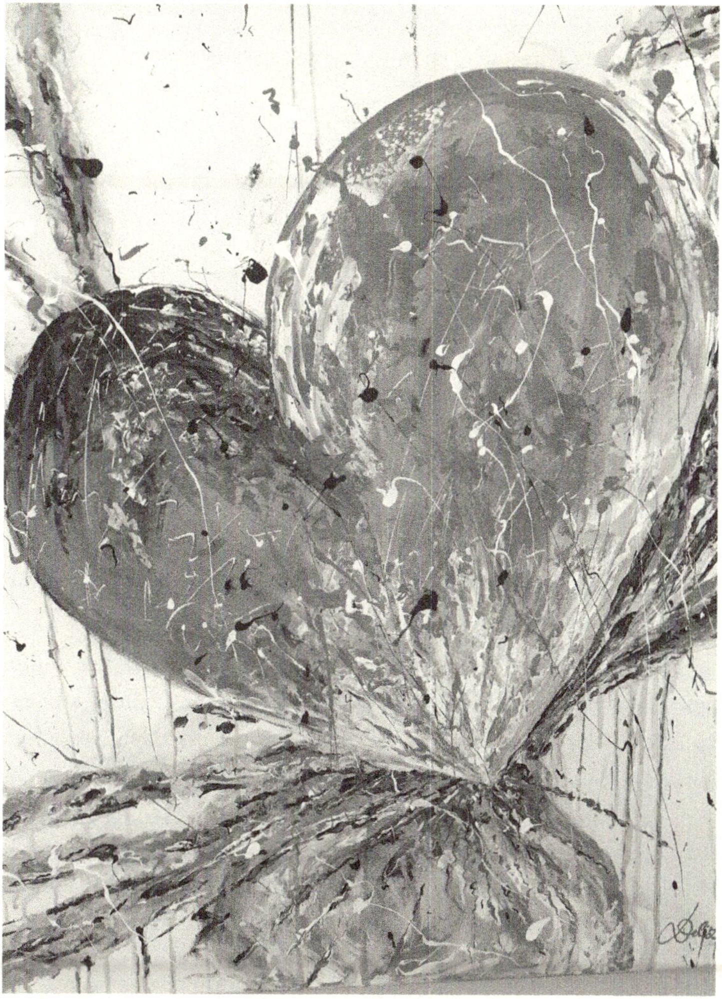

## PAGE 49

*To have loved this woman as deeply as I have is insane. To have felt this level of passion and desire for her, for this length of time, lacks reason. It is pure craziness. I have loved her more than I've loved anyone in my life. More than I've loved my own mother or my grandmother, my sisters, aunts, and cousins combined. And worlds more than I could ever love my wife. I've thought about this woman each and every day for one solid year. I have been with her in my mind each waking moment of the day and with her in my dreams at night. Oh, those blessedly vivid dreams, those subconsciously driven mirrors of the soul, where her essence, her moves, and her very being come to life. In my imagination – my endless fantasies – she has had every part of me. This perfect female is without equal. When she is in my sight, I am complete. Without her I am nothing.*

*To her, however, I do not exist.*

*And now she's...*

CROSS

We each drag a cross. Or more likely, a cross drags us. My cross is a daily, virtually unbearable commute to Boston. Every morning, the five-o-five leaves Haverhill inbound to the end of the line. The great engine moans as if it too shares in bearing the weight of the great cross of the commuter. With the creaking and grinding, and creaking and grinding, and creaking and grinding of hard metal against hard metal it moves the train from a sluggish crawl to a tentative jog. Finally, after what seems like most of an eternity, the great engine reaches full speed. We're moving as fast as a frightened rabbit. But then, curiously and with little warning, the long train slows even as the great engines, that did not want to pause, roar in protest. Oh no, no – it slows. No – it slows, slower it goes until reluctantly, it moves to a crawl, before it jerks to full stop.

Commuters board like robots accidentally caught in a mindless behavior that is not innate but programmed. They are driven to do something seemingly important, to go somewhere they've named destiny as they try to appear needed. Silently, they board and sit in a seat next to a seat, or in a seat next to the window, or next to the aisle. Sometimes they sit awkwardly and try not to stare at the face of a stranger. At this early stop they all have a padded seat on the train and sit they will.

Jerk. Lurch. Jerk. Tug. Lurch. The train moves with sounds of its metal-bottomed-cross heard dragging behind it. The all-too-cheery conductor is tossed from right to left to right again like a pendulum of an old grandfather's clock as he walks from front to back. His learned feet steady his strong right hand as it clutches firmly the all-powerful ticket puncher. Snap-snap. Done. Punched. The ticket is now worthless like the conductor's own pathetic, circular life that always ends where it started, day after tiresome day.

Full speed ahead moves the train, again.

And spare me the name of the next town and the view of the next town's dilapidated depot. No one is listening. Everyone is asleep. It's not even six yet the sun, oblivious to humans and their toils, rises nonetheless. This September sun sends its light streaming sneakily low across the warm platform of the next depot. Stopped yet again. More robots board. Some clutch the just delivered newspaper while others hold nothing but their phone in a feeble attempt to remain connected to someone who feels the same need.

There's one! Look, there is a true novice with her Styrofoam cup of petroleum-laced hot coffee held in high reverence like the Pope's scepter. Soon you will spill that little cup of coffee. That cup is your cross within a cross, you fool.

I'm going to lose my mind riding this train. Rail is right. Soon I'll go off the rails. I'll go loony on this old-time machine. Start. Stop. Start. Stop. Start. Stop. Stop. We're all going to go off the rails. We'll all surely derail. Just look at them. All of these people, now with no room to sit in a seat, stand instead. They hold on with one hand, or with both, to shiny poles lathered with fingerprints from hundreds that were there before them. Hang on and listen as the conductor gives the all clear. You hangers-on are one with the train. You will jerk-lurch again and again.

Snap-snap. Done. Punched.

Why are all of these people going to Boston? Are they going there to play perhaps? No. Not to play, not at this early hour. Are they going there to visit someone? No, if it was Saturday or a Sunday, then maybe yes, but not today. Definitely no. Not on a Monday or a Tuesday, not on a Wednesday or a Thursday and definitely not on a Friday. Are they going to work? Yes. All of these robots are going to work. What they do I do not know and, moreover, I do not care. I'd be a fool if I cared about them, and they would be equally foolish if they cared about me.

Look there. Just look at these people standing on this next platform waiting their turn to board the boredom train brimming with bums bound for Boston. Your only salvation is that you boarded closer to the end of the line, inbound. Your out has been everyone else's in to this point but your penalty, your payment for the lesser fare ride is that you have to stand. Stand up and hold on. No room for you. Squeeze in tight like floss between molars. Have a nice ride you short-ride-in-bounders; you sorry, lazy bunch that could've biked to North Station faster and have spared us long-ride-inbounders yet another painful cycle of stop and start.

Ever so slowly the massive engine with its string of cars full of packed workers crawls to a smooth but teasingly slow stop. A mere twenty feet from the huge bumper, a work-of-art, fail-safe gizmo designed to protect the terminal station from becoming bumped or bulldozed.

"Boss-ton!" proclaims the yo-yo conductor who is the first one to slam the door open and the first one in line at the donut shop. And like robots programmed to follow, we too leave the train with the short-riders off first and the long-riders off last. We debark the train as our preprogrammed script dictates; some of us even do so quite eagerly. The long trip or the short sleep is over and the next phase, whatever it may be, will, in comparison to what we've just endured, seems like, literally and figuratively, a reawakening. With briefcase in hand and weary eyes focused straight-ahead we boldly walk among the mayhem of modern-day humanity.

And who am I to judge the masses? I too join them on the workweek conveyor belt. Pathetic am I.

What awaits most of us at the end of the inbound ride? What is the reward for having survived the daily migration? Nothing less than to step from the burning coals directly into the molten lava, otherwise known as the outbound subway, or inbound subway depending on what the sign says. The oft-scolded little brother of the commuter rail is perpetually angry at the world and it shows us no mercy. Us robots, of course, are conditioned to ignore the violent screeches and whiplash-whooshes and jerks and more jerks on plastic seats custom molded to fit the bottom of the largest robot, a shape that allows all other robots to slide around freely like a pat of butter in a hot skillet.

∼

BLESSED ARE you that obey the opposite reaction to every given action rule – the end-of-the-day return trip of the faithful commuter.

This time it's the angry little brother that goes first. And, as usual, it is not in the mood to assist the now tired and weary robots that astonishingly sleep amid the violent jerks. Robots wake just in time to sleepwalk across the small platform to the larger, longer, more solid runway that lead to the big train. Announcements blaring overhead for the times and the tracks for the outbound trains go unheard; robots don't need to listen. Out of raw repetition they know where to go.

Now the robots are fast asleep on the outbound train. The click-clacker, who is no longer so sunny, moves along the rows and rows as the day's light fades to grey at the end of the day when the mighty engine finally sighs for a five-hour rest.

Hooray, I'm home. Home is a narrow, two-bedroom, ranch that requires more attention than I care to give it and to a wife that doesn't care about me nor the train with its click-clacker conductor, or of any of the stops, nor of the robots or of the train's angry little brother. Inbound to her has no meaning and outbound means less. Whether I am groggy with sleep from boredom or from life itself, like inbound or outbound commuters, means nothing to my first, and sadly perpetual, wife.

She means well if she means anything at all.

After a quick two hours filled with dinner, dishes, and suburban-life drama, I prop my cross by the bedpost and crawl into bed, alone.

## ME

*I* am a 30-year-old computer programmer for a large company nestled in Government Center off the Green Line E. I spend days sitting at a desk staring at four oversized computer screens. I debug software. The work is as impossible as counting snowflakes in a blizzard, but it's a job that at the end of the week yields a decent paycheck. This is what I'll be doing for the next three decades or so until I realize that my life has been totally wasted. Perhaps then I'll do something meaningful. Hopefully by then I'll be able to define meaningful.

I drink coffee until noon and tea from noon onward. I don't snack and I have lunch at exactly eleven thirty-five in the cafeteria. I don't gossip, waste time, surf the net, nor do I stare at or chat on my phone. I go to work, complete tasks until five in the evening when I leave for home.

Home is in Live Free or Die New Hampshire. It's a place where we do not live for free, but where I will certainly die. Perhaps the state's motto should be shortened to just: Die New Hampshire. By we I mean my wife and me. I've been married for five years and to this day I cannot remember what attracted me to her and I'm sure she could not say what she saw in me. We have a house that means we have a mortgage, and we own a car that means we have an auto loan. We have two geckoes that mean absolutely nothing at all, at least to me anyway. We don't have a garden, nor a deck or a swimming pool. Our neighbors are old and unfriendly. Our neighborhood bustled with children decades ago.

My wife has never held a job for more than a few weeks. She wanted to be a librarian until she realized that she dislikes books and disdains being around them. She then thought about being a sous chef, but she refused to work in a restaurant that served meat of any kind, seafood or GMO vegetables, so that idea ended after interviewing at three local restaurants. Last year, during the holidays, she worked as a cashier for an arts and crafts store, but that didn't last long either. The large number of small items people purchased overwhelmed her. She lashed out at those that bought more than 10 things at a time. She was fired the day after Christmas. She viewed these poor attempts at finding jobs not as setbacks, but as divine providence. On her own, and with no real membership to any religion, she proclaimed that God intended for her to stay home and to be a mother. One night she declared that she wanted us to start a family. She wanted at least two children, five at the most. When she broke this news to me, I gave her the same look I gave her when she wanted to move to the Philippines and start a business exporting coconut oil.

So far, divine intervention is alive and well in our house as my wife has yet to conceive a child despite numerous attempts over the years. Perhaps my sperm knows that I am less than enthusiastic about becoming a father.

We have developed a routine designed for childless couples. In the evenings we eat dinner, clean up, then we watch mindless television. We are asleep by nine. Weekends are spent paying bills, cutting the grass, taking in a movie or walking into town to eat lunch at the sub shop.

We tolerate each other as best we can as we toil in our plain vanilla lives. We patiently wait for each season to change.

Thank God for the changing seasons.

# FRIDAY

For some reason the train was jammed pack on this last Friday in September as it stopped at Melrose-Cedar Park. This is the second of three stops in Melrose. It must be a large town with a large population because a lot of people board the train in Melrose. Perhaps it's popular because it's so close to Boston? We're only two more stops, and a whole 15 minutes away, from North Station so Melrose may as well be Boston's baby sister, that's how close they are to each other.

As if it's been reserved for me all along, the fifth window seat on the right side of the first car behind the engine is where I sit. Each morning on the inbound ride that seat is mine. Everyone who boards the train in Haverhill at that early morning hour knows that that seat is taken, and they walk right by it to their own self-designated seat. A favorite seat on a commuter train is one of those silly games us robots play. I sit alone until we arrive in Reading when someone, usually a keep-to-oneself, CEO-type, occupies the adjoining aisle seat.

From my perch I have a clear view of the robots standing on the platform waiting to board. I recognized them by a particular item they carry on their back, or in their hand or by what they wear. Or I know them by their trade. Construction workers, electricians, plumbers, other laborers all fit the stereotypic blue-collar motif: rugged, loud, and carrying a Boston Herald newspaper. Students have ear buds firmly in place – they either type on their laptop if they have a seat, or if they stand they just listen to whatever they are listening to. Sharply dressed white-collar workers that are headed straight to the financial district uniformly read a paper such as the *New York Times*, *The Wall Street Journal*, or *The Boston Globe*. The rare weekday tourist simply stares at the list of stops posted on the wall near the exit and sheepishly hands their ticket to the all-too-cheery conductor.

Wait! Now wait a minute.

Who is this?

Who is this person about to board from sleepy Melrose-Cedar Park? I watch from above as she repositions her brown shoulder-length, wavy hair behind her ears with her left hand as she glances over her left shoulder at the sign that now displays the destination and departure time of the train she is about to board, as if she is confirming the existence of the train itself. I see her now standing by the entrance looking down the aisle, looking for something that is no longer exists – an empty seat. It is standing room only on this Friday, and not one of the aisle men are man enough to give up their seat for her. I am not surprised. These idiots never do.

She wraps her slender left arm around the vertical, stainless steel pole anchored to the floor of the aisle by the second row of seats, just three rows in front of me. I have a clear view of her big brown eyes as she takes stock of her immediate surroundings. I make sure to look away when her eyes pan in my direction. I don't want her to see me watching so I turn my eyes to the window. When I look back, I see that she has something in her hands.

The brunette with the wavy brown hair and brown eyes is gripping a book about the size of a small picture frame in her left hand. In her right hand, a pencil, an old fashioned, number 2 wooden yellow pencil that is shortened to about one-half its original length; the pink eraser is slightly rounded. I watch as she opens the book, moves the red ribbon place marker aside and begins to write. What is she writing? Is she jotting a note or recalling a memory? Could this be her diary? Would she be so daring as to open her personal diary in public?

---

> I've completely lucked out. I found him on my very first day, on my first ride into the city. How could I have been so fortunate? Fate – I don't believe in you but tempt me you do! Repeatedly you taunted me and today you've done it again, your pattern-free feathers tickle by entire body.
>
> Because I am standing, I can see him clearly. I have the same downwards gaze whether looking at this word or eyeing him. He has a window seat only a few rows back. For a thirty-something he has a young man's face – almost childish. His eyes are wide-set but I cannot see what color. He has sharp WASPy features with straight sandy hair parted on the left and combed to the right. Clean cut and neat. Perhaps he has some Irish in him? His jaw is angular and square, mouth small. His eyesight is near perfect because the lenses on his wire-framed glasses are very thin. I cannot tell if he is married, as I cannot see his hands. Do married men still wear wedding bands? He is casually dressed. My guess is that he's an accountant or perhaps he works at a brokerage firm. I bet he's shy and perhaps lonely too because he keeps sneaking glances in my direction. Dare I say he's looking at me? I wonder.

---

Malden Center, the final stop before the end of the line and the last of the robots board the train. Oh, no. No! Now she's surrounded, now my view of her is gone. Damn!

---

>I had to move slightly to be able to still see him, but obviously he can't see me. His head bobs in the air like a turtle's snout in and out of the water. Could he, could he be looking for me?

---

Where did she go? I'm sure she's somewhere in this river of commuters briskly making their way into North Station, but I don't see her. How could she have disappeared so quickly?

## WEEKEND

For as long as I can remember, I've loved the weekend. Since I was a kid, I always thought that everyone loved the weekends. No, I don't think it was my imagination, everyone seemed profoundly happier on the weekends. My dad worked Monday through Friday while my mom stayed home and took care of my sister and me. We were happy enough during the week, but everything just seemed lighter on Saturdays and Sundays; it seemed like life itself was somehow smoother and easier on those days too. The weekend usually began on Friday evening when an aunt or an uncle along with some cousins, or friends, sometimes both, would stop by our house. Some would play the piano, others would sing and dance and of course, everyone ate and drank. Even now, as a grown man with all of the responsibilities of a marriage, a career, a home with a list of repairs that seem to grow faster than weeds, I looked forward to the change from the hectic to sane, and to the more relaxed cadence and bliss of the two weekend days.

Until now, that is.

As I stepped off onto the Haverhill platform at the end of the outbound ride on this unusually memorable Friday, I can think only of one person – the woman I saw this morning with the wavy brown hair and brown eyes.

Of course, this is crazy. I don't know her. I don't know who she is or what she does. And I really didn't get a good long look at her either. Indeed, the only thing I do know is that she boarded the train at Melrose-Cedar Park and that she wrote in a small book in pencil. I may never see her again so why have I been thinking about her all day at work and during the entire ride home? And why do I think of her now? I probably will never lay eyes on her again. She probably won't be there on Monday. Monday? But what if she *is* there Monday? Monday is so far away? Weekends usually pass quickly, right? Please, please be a fast weekend.

∼

EIGHT O'CLOCK SUNDAY evening and I'm finally in bed. Sleep! Please sleep, come whisk me away and end this damn neverending weekend. I'm ready to rest for eight hours then wake at 4 a.m., bathe, groom, eat. I'll be in my car by 4:40 for the 15-minute ride to the depot. I'll step aboard the five-oh-five at exactly 5. I'll sit in the window seat, right side, five rows back. I can't wait until tomorrow.

Come on sleep, come.

## MELROSE-CEDAR PARK

*If* the engine is running smoothly and if tracks are clear then we should arrive at Melrose-Cedar Park in less than an hour, around 52 minutes. The overcast sky with on and off drizzle will not slow the train. Hurry everyone. Climb up and sit down. Let the clicky-clicker conductor yell the "All clear" so we can move on.

And why do we stop in Bradford? It's all of three whole minutes away from the Haverhill starting line. What a waste of energy, a waste of momentum. Come on. Come on people move it, move it. Take your seats and fall asleep.

Chop-chop.

Finally, we get some real speed. Lawrence. Lawrence is next. Christ! Look at the load on this platform. Is everyone eager to go to work today or what? All clear, right? Move it, move it. Andover's next then flagging the stop at Ballardvale and...and...damn...stopping for one idiot at Ballardvale. Really? Okay, remain calm. Flagging North Wilmington, good ole Wilmington, no one. What do they do in Wilmington anyway? Reading's next. Or is it Reading, like I'm reading a book? Lots of people here and usually someone takes this empty seat to my right. And, yes, right on cue. A blonde this time. I've seen her before, so I dutifully smile as if to say, "Hi. Have a nice day. Nice weather huh?" But I say nothing. I only smile. She's already rereading her last text message anyway.

Wakefield's crowded too. Move in. Back up. Make room. Melrose-Highlands. I better have a good look here. Maybe she'll board on this Melrose stop. Can there really be highlands in Massachusetts? Okay, stay alert. Next stop, Melrose-Cedar Park. It's always slow going through this town but we're now approaching the platform and there's a whole bunch of people most with hats and some with those useless little black umbrellas.

Wait. I think I see her.

Yes! There she is and she's wearing a hat.

Oh my god she is so... she was heading to the rear door, but she's turned and is heading towards the front as she did last Friday. She's taken her position at the same grab pole among the same group of pathetically seated males.

Would you just look at her? She is so adorable in that simple black rain hat. The hat's taupe underside accentuates her dark features. How lovely. She is even more attractive today than she was last week. Is that possible? I now see her face in profile, as she had to pivot about the pole to her left to make room for someone else. Stunning. If I had my camera, I would try to capture the curves of her face in silhouette, with her hat and its brim – so provocative alongside the ramrod straight metal pole – so alluring in profile. I can see the composition in my mind and I'm in love with it. Did I just think love? When I thought, I'm in love with *it*, as in the idea of the picture or did I mean that I'm in love with her? No, that can't be right, could it? If someone said to me, I love your scarf does it mean, I love you? With a deletion of that one last letter 'your' becomes 'you' so any compliment with the 'love your blank' becomes 'love you'. Is it a simple, subconsciously driven message?

She has her little book again, and she opened it. There's her pencil. She's looking straight ahead. What is she thinking? She's so wonderfully pensive. Look away you fool before she sees you watching her.

Admit it, you're infatuated. Tell me, Melrose...are you my love?

---

> He's exactly where I expected him to be, this man of routine who seeks order in a chaotic, sloppy world. Clearly, he's a sensitive type who appreciates the nuances between white and gray, and also between gray and black. Could he be lonely? I look at the advertisement above his window to see his eyes in the reflection. He has sad eyes. Perhaps he is lonelier than I first thought. A sensitive man? A lonely man?

---

Today, when she leaves the train, I will keep my eye on her. Just look for her black hat. Yes, there she is, up ahead. She's veering right, and she's gone. There are just too many people in this world.

You know that you are a fool, right? She may be lovely and perhaps even a nice person, but so what? What are the odds that you have something in common with her? Is it because you ride the same train? Work in Boston? Come on, don't be a sentimental idiot. Why would you care about someone you are never likely to meet? Someone who, in all likelihood, is not your type? After all these years could she be the woman of my dreams? No way, fool. It's like loving the petite meteorologist on television. It's just an illusion, not real and besides, you're married.

You can just stop this nonsense right here, right now.
No more.

---

I hope he's on the train tomorrow.

---

∽

IT'S TUESDAY, the first day of October and I am exhausted. Last night I dreamt a nightmare. The last thing I remember before falling asleep was that I didn't want to think about Melrose. She'd been on my mind all day. I again lost sight of her on the platform at North Station. How can she disappear so quickly? She seems to dive deeply in the sea of people and then she vanishes. One thing is clear. I am obsessed. Irrationally, irrevocably, obsessed. Who is she? Why am I drawn to her so?

Last evening, I decided that I wanted nothing more to do with her. I needed to get her out of my mind. She was driving me mad. Then I had that dream. It happened very late last night or early this morning; afterwards I was so restless that sleep was impossible.

In the too-real, dream, I was outside tending to the lawn when I looked over to the side door only to see Melrose standing at the stoop. My wife had just opened the storm door and she and Melrose said something to each other that I did not hear. Suddenly, and to my horror, my wife slapped Melrose on the left side of her face. The force of the hit knocked Melrose to the ground. Stunned, I froze. I could not move. Melrose appeared dazed and hurt. When I looked up at my wife, the horror turned tragic. The person standing at the storm door grinning with delight was not my wife at all. She was my mother. Not the nurturing mother of my youth, but the old person who now lives alone in elderly housing and whose memory consisted only of her last meal, if that. I cradled Melrose's head in my arms and stroked her fine hair. I awoke in a restless state of confusion and bliss. On one hand I was unsure what the dream meant; on the other, it was wonderful to have been with Melrose, to have come to her aid, to have comforted her, even under that imaginary circumstance.

Well, now that I've slept for most of this ride, I'd better wake up and straighten out because Melrose-Cedar Park is only two stops away.

And there she is again, and she is as lovely as ever. What I'd give to be able to talk with her, to hear her story, to watch her lips as she spoke. To learn what she enjoys, what she dislikes, what amuses her and what frightens her, to simply hold her hand. But these things may never happen. We are only passengers on a train. We will be strangers forever. Of that I am sure.

Where's my notebook?


*PAGE 1. I can hold back no longer. From this day forward, I will try my best to express my feelings for Melrose in writing. I will write them on paper, with this pen so I won't be able to erase what I wrote. Permanent feelings. I'll fold these pages and tuck them in the slit between the seat and the inside wall of the train, lost forever. Trashed. When she is in my sight I will write as my heart dictates. If my heart beats in frustration, words of discontent will fill this page; if it is filled with passion, the words of longing and desire will spill forth; if envious, then there is no telling what my heart will say if it is brave enough to say the truth. I have never been one to use to the written word, but in her presence I feel differently. A strange, foreign set of emotions takes over, as if I'm punch-drunk and dumbstruck at the same time. Love before Melrose was as predictable and as tacky as a dime store Valentine's Day card but now it is simply, well, it is simply love defined.*

---

He seems to be occupied today. His head is down. I cannot see what he is doing. Reading perhaps? He has barely looked up nor has he looked out the window. Strange.

---

# EXPRESSIONS

*Page 2. The dream I had the other night, when I held and comforted you in my arms, still haunts me. I see you now and amid the chaos that surrounds me, I will try to daydream. In this daytime dream, you are where you are at this moment but without the crowd that surrounds you. Indeed, the entire train is empty as it moves along the stable tracks unhindered by a next stop, a conductor nor an engineer. We are alone and we hear only the rhythmic sounds of travel. Despite the empty seats you are standing as you are right now; steadied by your left arm that is tightly wrapped around the pole. Your book is in your left hand and a pencil is in the right as usual. Boldly, tentatively, I approach you from behind. I gently hold each of your shoulders. You are expecting me, so you do not flinch, instead you turn your head to your right and meet my gaze. For a moment we look like the cover of one of those romance novels; our passion is deep and reciprocal. No words are spoken – they are not necessary, they are too trivial for the moment. Slowly I kiss the nape of your smooth neck. It is a single kiss that is held for a moment, a moment we both freeze with eyes closed. As the kiss ends, I worry. I think about kissing you again, but I don't. I am unsure of where that invisible boundary lies. Perhaps I've crossed it already, perhaps I'm not even close.*

Page 3.
*I need to say it... No!*
*I die to say it... Yes!*
*I want to say it... Don't!*
*Caution! Be damned!*
*Melrose, I love you!*
*There, at last!*
*Pent-up, unadulterated desire*
*And passion released.*
*I love you, I love you, I love you, alas.*

---

He seems to be writing. A writer has he just become? Or a writer he's always been?

---

Page 4.
*Last evening, I heard a love song, and you were there.*
*I heard the calling coos of the mourning doves at daybreak,*
*and you were there.*
*I saw a crimson maple leaf falling to the ground,*
*and you were there.*
*When I felt the sun's rays cut the autumn air, you were there.*
*So many things I share with you. Oh, how I wish you were here.*
*Silly.*
*You're right there, out of reach, so very far away.*
*Perhaps I should just ask you for one day?*
*Just one day to let you say that you mean no harm –*
*but stay away.*

*Is that what you'd like? Is that the message you'd convey?*
*"Be gone fool!" you'd say.*
*Go your own way.*
*Go back to your wife*
*To your married life.*
*A stifling strife where passion's on strike, now be gone fool.*
*Silly? No. No. No.*
*I must watch the flame, not pinch it out.*
*Keep it lit at all costs, even in doubt*
*Dreaming of a sun that may*
*Never rise.*
*A moon that may*
*Never set.*
*Stars with light from afar*
*Like your love*
*Afar.*

PAGE 10. *Excuse my giddiness, my liveliness, and my halting stammer as I try to reconcile who are you? Are you some sort of gift perhaps? My desires, wants and needs personified? Or are you a dream that will eventually become my heartache of a nightmare? Look I am writing these words because I must look down and pretend to not be interested in you when all I want to say is hi. Hello, my name is Jonathan Whipple. I work in Boston. I'm a computer programmer and I commute every weekday from New Hampshire. What is your name? I've nicknamed you Melrose. Sometimes I just call you Rose. Is that okay? It is a lovely name, would you agree? It seems to suit you because it is unique. What I mean is that it seems like you are unique in that you are writing in your book when everyone else is doing something other than writing, so in that sense, you seem to be unique. I very much would like to ask you questions because you intrigue me. I'd like to know everything about you, yet I do not want to frighten you or to make you think I'm some kind of nutcase because that is not who I am at all. Am I making any sense to you? In my mind I've had several conversations with you, and you are the only one who could tell me if you are who I think you are. In my mind, you are perfect. Are you perfect? A perfect Rose?*

---

He walks away from the train with furrowed brow as if in deep thought, oblivious to his surroundings. He's on autopilot as he heads into North Station.

---

*Page 17. Today, for the first time, I clearly saw your eyes. They are light brown and wide set. Black pupils with sharply defined hazel irises set against pure white that lack those common red cobwebs of distress. They are not sad eyes or mad eyes, but eyes that are clearly focused and determined. Someday I'd love to stare deeply into your eyes, to study the unique pattern of your irises, to watch how they twitch slightly around the pupil. I love your eyes, Rose.*

*Rose, you look like someone who is in control of your day and your destiny. You look sure of your ways. Are you? As I see you at this very moment it seems as though you've had a nice weekend. Perhaps you spent time with someone who was intimate with you? Perhaps someone who made you feel like lovemaking was nothing more than second nature when he (or she perhaps) was with you. In my mind you are a kind and gentle person who loves to be loved. Can I assume you are heterosexual? Yes, I will assume that for now, but it would not bother me at all if you loved women too. Why, you ask? Because anyone, anyone at all, able to experience your touch would be blessed with good fortune, foremost among them me.*

We locked eyes! For a brief moment our eyes spoke to each other. My eyes remained quiet while his screamed jumbled sentences filled with words that seemed shocked to have been summoned into action at that moment. His face cried for more, but his eyes turned away suddenly. Did he do so in an effort to shield his heart, perhaps?

---

*Page 24. This morning I awoke with my heart racing. I dreamt that you were no longer here. That you did not get on the train as you always do. That you just disappeared. I cried, "Wait, don't go. When will I see you again? Where? Please tell me where. I'm not good with loss. Did I lose you?" When did I become this way? Crazed about a stranger. No. Thankfully you are here as you've always been. I love Melrose-Cedar Park. I love you Rose. I'm so tired.*

---

He doesn't look well today. Perhaps he's fallen ill? His head is buried in his arms and he is leaning forward against the seat in front of him.

---

*Page 25. During this cold, sorrowful season of misplaced joy and painful, twisted memories I ask, why her and why now? Happy new year to you, my Rose.*

*Page 26. You fill my senses as I wade through this river of desire so long foreign to me.*

*Page 33. Do I hear you say things to me? Words I've yearned to hear from someone who cares about me but who is not my blood? Do you say them in jest to tease me or do your words, as I hope, spawn from your heart? And what of my heart – that wretched muscle that has been stretched and pulled and torn and divided that until now only bled for my family. Pray tell – what of my aging heart?*

Page 41.
*It's spring, the weather's warm!*
*Let's skip today and run off together, we'll hold hands and talk,*
*we will...*
*Skip tomorrow too and we'll get married and have children,*
*we will...*
*Skip ahead to when our children have children that will visit us,*
*we will...*
*Skip to a time when we can barely walk, when we reminisce*
*about that first day when we ran off together,*
*we will...*
*Oh! To live those wild, whimsical stages of life with you, Rose.*
*Will we?*

# EMPTY SOUL

*Page 50.*
*All of the words have been written*
*All sonnets sung*
*My own heart yearns still*
*Love, will you ever come?*
*You were*
*My life*
*My passion*
*My day*
*Your very existence led me astray*
*Now you've left me, Rose*
*A shell of a man in total disarray.*
*Forever I'll be lost*
*For never again, I fear*
*Will I open my pathetic...*
*My pathetic*
*Empty soul.*

GONE

*D*ay after day followed by week after endless week, Jonathan Whipple tried to remain calm.

At first, he rationalized Melrose's absence as simply as possible. For the most part, he was determined to stay positive. From the late-spring through the summer months, he envisioned her on a sandy beach somewhere in the Caribbean enjoying the warm winds and clear blue waters. And despite the difficulties in imagining that others were enjoying her by either making love to her, or by holding her hand, or by just talking with her, Jonathan quelled those jealousies by accepting the premise that if they were correct then she'd still be alive. And that he'd see her again.

Of course, she could also have left town to be with someone who needed her. Someone like her mother perhaps, or her father or another family member, a friend perhaps. He imagined Melrose with an immense heart and endless empathy; the type of a person who was selfless, giving, caring – someone who could soothe a deep pain or support a crippled soul by simply being there.

There were times, especially in the dark, early morning

hours as Jonathan lay in bed next to his wife, when his mind considered that something bad happened to Melrose. Not surprisingly his thoughts on her potential misfortunes swung wildly, from having suffered a true, but non-life-threatening case of influenza, to something fatal such as a rare, aggressive cancer. The more he tried to dismiss those thoughts the more his mind ratcheted up the virulence of the disease. The runaway cycle spun so wildly that it ultimately drove him from his bed in a maddened and delirious state.

It was the commute following those endless nights when Melrose's absence disturbed Jonathan the most. It was on those days when sound reasoning yielded to despair, when he poured out the remaining contents of the proverbial half-filled glass, leaving it unequivocally empty. He loathed those days.

Jonathan plodded on, month after cruel month, half-heartedly at best. Even the dual seasons of joy and renewal that encompass the second half of December through the first days of January seemed to mock him. There was no joy in his world. No bells, no magic. And while he questioned whether or not Rose even qualified as an acquaintance, he knew full well that he didn't want her to be forgotten and she will always be brought to mind. Auld Lang Syne was nothing but another reminder of her absence, a frivolous jingle to be quietly dismissed.

∽

TEN MONTHS HAVE COME and go and still no sign of Melrose, still no sign of hope, and still no sign that anything was going to change. Jonathan noted that the clicky-clicker did his thing seemingly unfazed by Melrose's absence and all of the other robots did their thing too, with nary an ounce of concern. And why would they notice? All the tickets look the same to the clicky-clicker and everyone else simply worried about themselves; they were oblivious to a fault.

A full year's worth of seasons had passed without as much as a peek, nor even mirage of Rose. Jonathan had resigned himself to the reality that she was gone forever – a reality that was unbearable.

It was springtime again. The air was noticeably different, the greens were greener, and the sun shone longer. These changes mattered to most people, but not to the commuter who sat in the fifth window seat on the right side of the first car behind the engine.

It seemed like any other day, that near-summer day when Jonathan stepped off the train and walked into Boston's North Station.

## LOVE'S AUTHOR

At first, he just stood and stared.

The memory circuits in Jonathan's brain flashed quickly as they sought to comprehend the presentation and to place the image. The cardboard display stand was designed not to be missed. The words were in bold print: "She's done it again! All praise Pendleton." – New York Times. "Love has meant so little, until now." – AllReaders.com. "Pendleton owns unrequited love." – The New Yorker.

The hardcover books were neatly tucked into each of the six nooks of the temporary display. On the display's header, in the bottom left hand corner, was a picture of author of the New York Times bestseller. She did not age a day since Jonathan last laid eyes on her. Rose's smile was tentative and pensive as it was many mornings on the five-o-five. Her lovely eyes, still clear and sharp, looked past the photographer to a distant object.

The jumbled sounds that emanated from the comings and goings of the crisscrossing crowd in North Station went silent as Jonathan walked closer to the display. He was in a world unto himself. Although he was not sure what he would do once he picked up a copy, he did so anyway and without hesitation. In a way he felt as if he was holding the author Victoria Pendleton herself.

A few sentences on the back of the book hinted at the secrets inside:

> *What happens when you finally see true love but it's not yours to have? When it's within reach but cannot be held? When it's genuine and true, yet untapped and fleeting? Melrose's mind instantly released soothing thoughts to protect her fragile soul. But it was too late. Her heart exploded and her mind followed. She became someone else altogether. Obsessed. Possessed. Relentless. She became* Love's Author. *Her words had an effect on everyone, everyone except the one man who truly loved her. And they haunted him forever.*

Jonathan felt his heart pounding through his chest when he read the name of the story's protagonist. How could Victoria have known about Melrose? What did she mean by possessive? Who exactly did Melrose become? Obsessed? Obsessed with what? With whom?

The new book opened naturally to the middle, which happened to be page 115, the beginning of a new chapter. Chapter 8 was titled: *Subconsciously*, and it began with a partial quote, ... *I awoke with my heart racing*.... Jonathan then closed the book and again opened it to an earlier chapter. Chapter 2 was titled, *Wistful*, and it too began with a partial quote, ...*our passion is deep and reciprocal*.... That each chapter began with a partial quote was odd yes, but within the realm of artistic creativity. It wasn't until Jonathan read the quote of the last chapter, did he make the stunning connection.

Ever since Rose stopped boarding the train to Boston, about one year ago, he truly has been lost, even haunted, one might say. Indeed, the quote that foreshadowed the book's final chapter was completely accurate for he has been ... *a man in total disarray*.... How could his own words, words he clearly recalled writing clumsily on the train, end up in this book by this prize-winning author known as Victoria Pendleton? Jonathan had kept his thoughts purposefully private. He tore each piece of that cheap-lined notebook paper that contained his innermost private feelings from its binder and made sure it was discarded. He did it himself.

Standing in front of the cardboard display, holding a first edition of a novel written by a woman he loved and lost without ever speaking a word to her, who appeared to have read his mind and heard his heart, was simply overwhelming. Jonathan was unsure of what to do next. Did he want to read this book? No, not really. Would he love to read the book? Yes, very much so. Could he live without it? Perhaps, but not easily.

"That will be twenty-two dollars. And you're the first to buy one today."

Jonathan handed the salesperson the money and placed the pristine copy of *Love's Author*, already a New York Times best-seller by Victoria Pendleton in a plastic bag.

"Enjoy it."

"Oh, it's not for me. It's for my wife. Today is our wedding anniversary. Until now I had no idea what to get her."

MANY EVENINGS, Jonathan would look at the postage stamp-sized photograph of Victoria on bottom left of the book's back cover. He'd then open the book to the second to last page and re-read the last line, having soon committed it to memory: *The author lives a simple life in New England with her dogs and cats. She travels often and enjoys riding trains.*

# EPILOGUE

"Good morning Ms. Pendleton."

"Why, good morning George. Another lovely day, wouldn't you say?"

"Indeed, it is. Indeed. Have you been away ma'am? It seems like a year since I saw you last."

"Why, yes George, how thoughtful of you to remember. I was on the five-o-five back then."

"Right. So, you were. Haverhill line, indeed, you were. Indeed."

And as he'd done countless time over the years, George, the conductor who had previously worked the Haverhill Line, removed Ms. Pendleton's round-trip ticket and, with a magician's smooth, sleight of hand motion, replaced it with a piece of paper that was folded neatly in thirds. No sooner had the chads from the punched Fairmont ticket to Readville landed on the floor of the mostly empty train did the bestselling author read the latest entry to her next novel, clumsily written words from another longing heart.

## THE END

# HATE

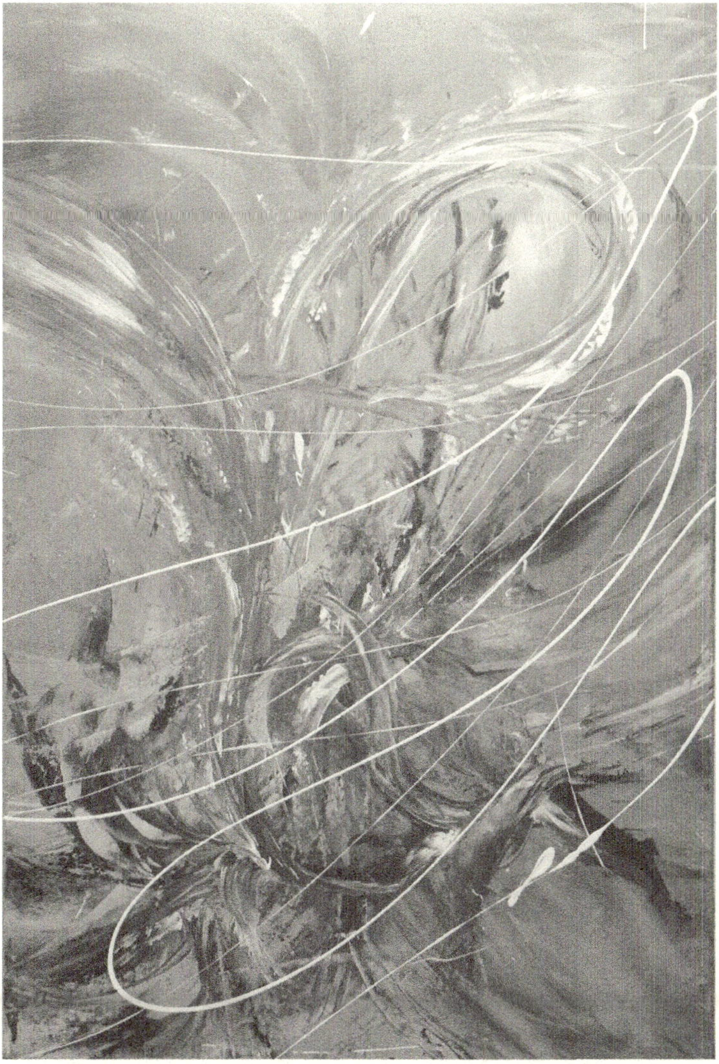

# WORD

It is a word that leaves no traces of doubt. It is as pure as it is simple. It is as powerful as an earthquake and as visible as a tornado. It goes straight to the heart. And it cuts deeply and cleanly like a scalpel with its sharp pinpoint tip and long thin edge; an instrument that lives for the exact moment to be deployed.

It is without equal. And its opposite is mistakenly so; it's antonym cannot subdue, mask or substitute the word's greatness.

It is one with its owner. Together they are vile, voracious and vapid.

It is ubiquitous but not unique.

It is as old as fire and as pervasive as the oxygen that fuels it.

It breeds through other words and it travels though humans amid their self-serving, purposeful deeds.

Hate.

Pure, unabashed, unbound, unrelenting, untainted hate.

Unfortunately, I've been forced to love it.

# LOGIC

Logic is sound in the mind possessed.

"We must do this for what we believe in. Our cause is just," he said to his younger brother. "Through our actions we will show the world that our way is righteous and absolute; their way is wrong. It degrades us. And at the end, we will prevail, and they will join us. Our cause is worth the fight."

"Through our childhood, you have always been right. You have shown me the way when I was lost and unfocused. You are my older brother; my blood and I will march with you; you know I will. But I must ask again, is there no other way?"

"Never, never, never, never, never again question me! Never again! You must do as I say and do not think you know more than me. Watch and learn. It is the way of our sacred world. Soon they too will know the path to redemption."

"True, brother. I know you are right. I will do what you say. I am the fight. But must we kill for others to see the light? Is there any other way? One that is less painful?"

"You test my patience, don't tempt my will. I will do as I must, they will be maimed and killed so they see our true way. I know these people. For them to understand, they must experience pain and grief and agony. The plan is simple. It will work, you will see. My bomb will go off first, here, then, your backpack will detonate later. Leave it here. See here? There will be people, but don't look at them and don't think too much. Just leave the pack then turn and walk away as I tell you. The runners will be the show, not you nor me. And remember, they are cowards. That is why they run. You are not a coward you do not run. Do not run. Do not think. Just do as I say. Walk fast. No one will know you. They will not be looking at you. They will be lost. They are always lost."

## GHOSTS

*J*ournalists were not allowed in rooms of the victims unless given permission by the patient.

"You're from the paper, right?"

"Yes."

"And you've written a lot of stories about a lot of things, right?"

"Yes, that's true."

"Do you believe in what you do? The stories you write? What you see and what you hear?"

"Yes. But I think I'm the one who should be asking the questions," she said nervously hoping to not upset the young runner who was still heavily medicated three full days after the bombs detonated and shattered everything near them.

"You can ask me all of the questions you want in a minute," he answered dryly. "But first you have to answer this one last question for me."

"Okay, shoot."

"Do you believe in ghosts?"

"In ghosts?"

"Yes, ghosts."

"Why do you want to know if I believe in ghosts?"

The young runner pulled back the sheets of his hospital bed to expose the heavily bandaged stump of what remained of his left leg. It looked like a silkworm's cocoon, and it was large enough to encase a puppy.

"Do you see my leg?"

The journalist saw what was left of the runner's leg. The thigh was bandaged from just above the knee to just below the groin.

"Yes, I do."

"My calf, my foot?" The journalist had only one honest answer. "No. No, I don't."

"That's strange because I do. I see it. I see my foot, my lower leg, and my upper leg with its big muscle. It's the same leg I crawled with as a baby, and it is the first leg I stood on when I was only seven months old. It's the same leg I used to pedal my tricycle, and my road bike. It's the same one I had when I kicked the winning field goal in high school and the exact one I often used to trip my sister. I grew up with that left leg. I dated women and I ran track with that left leg, and today I am glad that I can still see it and feel it too. When I reach over that big bandage, I can still feel it. But they tell me what I'm feeling is not real. They tell me that what I'm seeing is a ghost leg except I don't believe in ghosts or even in parts of ghosts. Just like you, I don't believe in ghosts. Right? Do you believe in ghosts?"

# AGHAST

*O*lder writers, those hardened souls whom have been in the business since the beginning of the Vietnam war, could handle the pain of interviewing survivors of tragic events. They were familiar with the look but when the young journalist saw that look in that one father's eyes, she immediately broke down. Later that evening, after dulling her pain with wine, the young journalist wrote in her personal journal:

---

> His focused-on-nothing, straight ahead gaze will haunt me forever. The love of his life, his son, was dead, the love of his life, his daughter, was maimed, and the love of his life, his wife, was badly injured. It seemed like he could not comprehend the full gravity of the moment. The moment was unexpected, and its impact immeasurable. Time for this father, for this husband, for this man stopped because the ability to string together rational thoughts failed. Time was suspended. I could not carry out my assignment. I had to leave. I did not want to be in

his line of non-sight. He was covered in blood and in disbelief. He was aghast.

---

## GUILTY

The courtroom was silent as the juror, who spoke for the entire jury of so-called peers of the accused, rose and faced the judge.

"With due respect to the court, and to the judicial system of the United States of America, we the jury would like to go off-script to make one thing clear. After two solid months of listening to testimony from eyewitnesses, victims, the family of victims, the defendant's lawyers and having witnessed the childish face of the accused exhibit nothing but contempt for the process and absolutely no remorse whatsoever for his self-confessed actions, your Honor, we the members of the selected jury who are white, black, brown, yellow, gay, straight, male, female, trans, young, and old, we unequivocally do not want to be considered a peer of the accused. He has no peers in our civil society, except with those who reside in their own morbid world of destruction. We find the defendant guilty of each and every charge of terrorism and murder. Moreover, your Honor, we unanimously support the death penalty for this waste of a human being. As he has killed without remorse, we too have no remorse in our decision."

"You are condemned to one thousand deaths young man!" proclaimed the judge. "Leave my courtroom, leave this city and the day could not some soon enough when you leave this world."

BEFORE THEY LEFT THE COURTHOUSE, again without their client who had been taken, shackled by both wrists and ankles, to a maximum-security prison where supper awaited, the legal defense team of the now convicted terrorist filed an appeal for a mistrial and also a plea to spare the killer's life based on the fact that he wasn't thinking clearly when he did the horrific things he did. "Why kill him," they reasoned to the weary judge. "He's just a young man who lost his way one day. He'll have better ones, we promise. We'll show him the way. Prison will be good; in it he'll thrive. To kill him will prove nothing. Why not just keep him alive?"

The old judge thought for a moment. He considered the plea and said quite rapidly, "Okay, okay, you have exercised your sway. But in one year's time come back, now please, be on your way."

And with those words, the killer survived his killings while his victims were either dead and buried, or alive to suffer or to mourn – hearts broken, lives shattered, dreams destroyed – muscle and tissue and tendons ripped, shredded, torn.

# UNWANTED SEED

Jack didn't look for trouble nor did he seek to wake up each day feeling as he now does. But it's too late. The unwanted seed had been sowed and its fruit only grows larger and riper with time. It is fair to say that there was a time in Jack's life when all that mattered could be summed up in just two words: wife and daughter. He loved his wife without pretense, and he absolutely adored his only daughter. Quiet, thoughtful, honest and nonjudgmental were traits he and his wife shared and qualities they directly passed to their child as if there was no other possible outcome. The young family went about their daily lives without intruding on anyone in any way, and for fifteen peaceful years no one intruded on them.

Then, in one short day, without warning, all of that changed.

"Are you sure you want to hear this?"

"Yes," replied Jack with his wife seated by his side.

"Are you absolutely sure you want to know these details? It won't change anything, you know that, right?" implored the medical examiner.

"Yes, we know."

And with a deep sigh, the short, overweight medical examiner began to read his report in a calm, unwavering voice as if he was reciting a poem by a well-known poet. "The victim was a female approximately 22 years of age. She was repeatedly struck about the head and face. Her breasts were bruised and bloodied, and she was forcefully raped. The victim was naked when she attempted escaped. She was shot twice, once in her right leg, and once in her right buttock at relatively close range. She bled as she ran for about twenty yards east towards the highway when the third, fatal bullet entered the back of her neck. The impact of that bullet nearly severed her head from her body. It is likely she died instantly at that point, but it is also plausible that she experienced a great deal of pain before she died of blood loss."

The medical examiner, a lifelong friend of the victim and the victim's family, added, "God almighty. I am so sorry. So very sorry."

The words, including the medical examiner's 'sorrys', seemed wooden.

It no longer mattered to Jack that his wife, who was sitting next to him, had to hear the sordid details. It was a foregone conclusion that they could no longer remain a couple. The site of each to the other was simply too painful to bear. It was better for them to separate, to simply disappear and pretend like the last twenty years didn't ever happen.

Jack turned to face the sheriff who leaned somberly against the wall by the door.

"Kip, would mind if I had a word with him?"

"Jack, you know I can't do that. He'll be facing the judge tomorrow, you'll be able to see him then."

"I know you remember all of those defensemen I stopped from reaching you Kip, when we played ball. And I haven't asked you for anything ever since we left that school Kip. But now I'm asking. I just want a word with him. I want to see him, and I want him to see me."

～

JACK WATCHED the boy inmate in Cell X through the monitors and imagined how the film of his first encounter with his daughter's rapist looked to his wife, or to anyone who bothered to view it. The department's clunky old video camera recorded the entire scene.

～

THE DEPUTY SHERIFF escorted the alleged rapist and murderer into the small interrogation room and seated him at the table across from Jack and his wife, who instantly froze in place. The tall, thin, shackled suspect with a tattoo in his right arm that read 'Bikers Rule' could not have been more than twenty-five years old, but his spoken words exposed a person whose brain was decades younger.

"Oh, is this the pretty mommy? And is this big man daddy?" he said sarcastically. "Are you the one that fucked that little twat before I got a piece of that candy? Hmm? Are you, daddy-o, daddy?"

Just as the gall of the suspect took Kip and the deputy sheriff by surprise, they were equally unprepared for Jack's measured response. Initially Jack sat motionless, head down with his hands folded on the table; he did not look at the suspect when he entered room. But at the third utterance of "daddy" it happened and in an ironic twist that word of endearment would be the last one the suspect would say with a clear voice for the rest of his life.

Within seconds, two things happened to Jack. The first was a ground swell – a collective consolidation within his body of a lifetime's worth of pent-up anger from times as a skinny child when he was ridiculed, or teased, or told that he wouldn't amount to much, from other times when he just listened and cried and endured the shove to the ground. The second event was directly attributable to the thousands of snaps of the football that the former high school star center made over his youthful career, a repetitive motion that resulted in a faster than normal upward reflex of his dominant right arm.

With a strike that would have made a viper envious, the enraged and distraught father's right hand grasped the slim throat of the thin suspect with a powerful fury. The force was such that the obvious intersection of the larynx and trachea was instantly and decidedly crushed, a shock that made the suspect's eyes bulge from its sunken, shallow sockets.

"I am your hell," Jack hissed at the suspect before extending his right arm fully, a move that pushed the thin rapist and murderer to the floor and onto his back.

～

As the memory of that life-altering encounter that occurred over a decade ago faded Jack looked over to the right of the large console at the video feed from Cell Z. There he saw the convicted rapist and murderer lying in a fetal position and shivering periodically on the cement slab in the cement room from where he rarely left. He was twelve years into serving a life sentence, but he wouldn't make it that long, not even close. The convict no longer ventured from the confines of the cement cell to the spacious living room with the large sofa and wall-mounted television. Instead he opted to remain in the relatively peaceful confines of the small stone cell. The wiseass hadn't gained wisdom over the years, but in a move that reflected his true nature, he gnawed off with his teeth most of the letters that had been artfully tattooed on his arm. Peeled often, the seeping and puss-filled scabs separate the four remaining letters: the first two of the first word and the last two of the other. Accurately labeled, the convicted rapist and murderer of Jack's only daughter and destructor of his first and only marriage no longer vacillated from temporarily sober to decidedly drunk. Rather he was now firmly placed at the very end of a different tangent all together, with little company, in the acrid, bile pit of hell.

## CELL X

The maximum-security prison in Colorado was designed to serve a single purpose: to isolate those convicted of the most heinous of crimes. Each cell had a room within a room. The cement and steel-reinforced outer walls of the seven by twelve-foot inner chamber sported an all-important four-inch wide window that served, at times, to be the only light the prisoner had during the day or night. Within these walls was a small foyer where one could become sandwiched between a sold steel door and iron bars that retracted open. The foyer was a passageway between the inner and outer chambers. The nondescript inner chamber was kept at a constant temperature of 72 degrees unless it rose to 100 or fell to 0, or just slightly below 0. It also contained a solid, immovable, stone gray concrete stool with a matching table and bed. The stainless-steel sink and toilet, compassionately bolted to the wall near the retractable iron bars, were positioned diagonally opposite the far corner of the room where the in-ceiling shower head was directly above the in-floor drain. The shower water was turned on for 5 minutes each day at random times without warning. Meals varied from cold to hot, and like the shower water, they arrived at random times of the day. At times the food was delivered when the water in the shower flowed.

The potential for someone to escape from this prison was nil given the 100 cameras and alarms, as well as the redundant isolation and segmentation measures. In addition, the prison was situated in the middle of 600 acres of desolate land. It was tens of miles from the nearest neighborhood, yet the residents of that small community pledged their willingness to take aim, and to effectively take out, anyone who sought to escape – a proclamation read to each new inmate upon arrival, and repeated weekly throughout the facility by use of its extensive sound system. Most of the townsfolk were eager for an escape to occur and some even suggested to officials that an inmate should be released one day, as a sort of a drill. To reinforce the premise that the community will back up federal authorities, all of the adult-sized, human shaped paper targets at the local shooting range were orange in color and emblazoned with the letters A-D-M-A-X to simulate the dress code of the prisoners.

Despite the enthusiasm of the town folk to take up arms for their country's local prison, it would not be necessary. The newest convicted terrorist would never step foot in any part of Colorado, or anywhere for that matter.

∽

THE BLACK DESK phone with the square push buttons was only a single line and only one person knew its number. Not even the local telephone company had a record of the line's existence. Direct communication made for efficient exchanges and no errors.

"Boston will arrive tonight. Which one?"
"Cell X."
"Copy."

∽

THE HIGHWAY in that corner of Wyoming ran on such a true east-west direction that many truck drivers, who sped along at 75 miles per hour for over 300 miles, were able to relax and have dinner with both hands once they locked their steering wheels in position. And that high rate of speed wasn't fast enough. The armored vehicle that transported the convicted Boston bomber caught up to, then passed, not one but several 18-wheelers in the dark of night. They were scheduled to arrive at the facility at exactly 0200, and to reach that goal meant the vehicle containing the driver, two heavily armed guards, and the shackled, convicted terrorist, needed to travel at 110 miles per hour for 90 minutes. Although the speeding armored vehicle was not a common occurrence, the local law enforcement authorities expected to see it every now and again and so it was, on this particular evening, no one bothered to tell local authorities of the transfer. Before the nearest town's sole patrol car left the station later that same morning, the delivery assignment would be completed.

There was no indication that the dirt road that led to Cell X was just up ahead. To the untrained eye, the right-hand turnoff looked like everything else in that desolate area – dessert-like terrain with patches of short, sparse, wild grasses that resembled randomly placed hair plugs on a bald man's head.

The wild, bumpy ride down the unmarked, 15-mile-long dirt road woke the Boston bomber. His seat on the truck's unpadded solid steel floor relentlessly foreshadowed the events that lay ahead.

A single 40-watt light bulb illuminated the back entrance to the single level building. The armed guards led the now hooded terrorist, who was thankful just to be standing, beyond the back-door entrance, down a well-lit lengthy corridor, through a thick solid steel door, and then through a small foyer to a room separated from the foyer with thick steel bars. One of the guards, a former Marine, removed the foot shackles, then the hand shackles, followed by the convict's hood. The former Marine's stiff elbow, delivered squarely to the unsuspecting convict's jaw, sent the terrorist reeling to the cement floor. There he lay in the dark in the back corner of the cell below the showerhead.

The armed guards backed out of the cell and the building. They reentered the armored vehicle, promptly returned to a remote airplane hangar and back to where their journey began six hours ago. The transfer team met its time deadline without incident. Their decade-long string of successful transfers remained intact.

~

THE CONVICT WAS STILL LYING on the floor of the shower when he heard the familiar voice of the CNN reporter. The low-level light that entered the concrete cell from the small window situated on the same wall from where he was now propped illuminated the small concrete cell. But it was the light streaming in from directly in front of him, from an area beyond the metal bars and the foyer and even beyond the steel door that was blinding. It took the Boston bomber a few moments to realize that there was nothing to stop him from leaving the confines of the small cement room. Astonishingly, he neither saw nor heard anyone; he appeared to be alone.

Slowly he stood. His mouth was parched, his jaw ached, and he felt dizzy and mildly nauseous. Looking to his left he saw the rest of the raw concrete room including the stainless-steel sink and toilet. There were no faucets on the sink and the small holed toilet was dry. Indeed, there was no water to be found anywhere in the cell. Tentatively, the marked young man walked toward the foyer. Neither the bars behind him, nor the steel retractable door now in front of him, moved. What he saw beyond the steel retractable door shocked him.

∽

OUTSIDE, on the surface of the desolate landscape, the small, square, red-bricked structure looked like any municipal water building. Indeed, the rusty sign in front of the chain-linked fence said as much and offered nothing more. Far below the small building, however, was a vast room accessible by a helical steel staircase that spiraled down thirty feet. The location and layout of the below ground bunker was known only to two people, but it was occupied on a constant basis by only one of them. The bunker housed not only the necessities of modern living – a full kitchen, a living room, a bedroom – but all of the technological advances made within the past decade, as well as those that would not be known to society for at least another decade. Ten quantum-based computers installed years ago, were perched on the continuous desk along three walls. Above the bank of computers were 50 medium sized, high-resolution monitors most of which were connected to remotely located cameras. The bunker was the center hub of three spokes. Cell X was at 0 degrees to the North, Cell Y was 60 degrees South-South east, and Cell Z was 120 degrees South-Southwest of the bunker. Although all three units were identical each was unique in its capacity to interact with its occupant, or on rare occasions, its occupants.

On this day, Jack was focused mainly on one guest, but it was one that he had eyed patiently and had prepared for over the course of a year. Like a python that hovered just below the surface of the water, he was ready to make the first of many moves but unlike the silent serpent Jack often spoke in his bunker. While no one heard him, Jack heard every sound made in the three cells.

"Hello, little boy Boston. What do you see?" Jack said as he watched the bewildered inmate survey the surroundings outside of the inner cement cell.

The relatively large room outside the inner cell looked like it belonged in a luxury condominium. A rather large television was mounted on the tall, smooth finished wall to the left of the room. CNN was broadcasting breaking news on the transfer of the convicted Boston marathon bomber to a high-level security prison in Colorado. The inmate walked over to the long couch that faced the television, sat on its soft cushions and listened to details of his own exit from Massachusetts. He tried to move the coffee table situated in front of the couch to provide easier access to the couch, but it did not budge. While the CNN coverage of the transfer shifted from the studio to an affiliated reporter standing outside a Supermax high containment facility – where they thought the convicted terrorist was housed – the inmate rose from the couch and looked out through the sliding glass door that effectively created the far wall of the room opposite the steel door entrance to the tiny cement cell. He cautiously gripped the handle of the sliding glass door and pulled it to the left.

For the second time that morning, the inmate was surprised. The door easily glided open and fresh air poured into the room. It appeared as though the only thing that stopped him from running out to the expanse of desert land was his own apprehension; there was not a fence nor a wall nor a barrier of any sort to be seen. He wanted to run as fast as his wildly beating heart could accommodate but, instead, he took a slow, tentative step across the threshold.

"Predictable," Jack said as he watched the inmate make the cautious move.

Because the inmate's head angled downward, it was a small lock of his curly brown hair, that looked nice on magazine covers but lacked pain-sensing nerve endings, that burned instantly as it came in contact with the invisible high voltage energy grid. The boy didn't smell the smoke from his hair for if he had it might have prevented him from coming into full contact with the grid. The energy from the grid threw him back into the room with such a force that cracking sounds were clearly heard by Jack as the small of the boy's back met the padded arm of the immovable black leather sofa.

Jack watched emotionless as the inmate grabbed his back and writhed in pain on the false wood ceramic-tiled floor. With a tap of the button on Jack's large console, the real-time breaking news was seamlessly usurped with a previously recorded CNN report of timeline of the Boston marathon bombing. Another knob on the console lowered the volume of the bunker speakers that carried the inmate's renewed shrieks as the young convict touched the long, thin burn marks on his forehead that immediately puffed out like small pink pillows, later to become translucent fluid-filled blisters.

"Let me guess. You will explore the refrigerator next. Are you hungry little Boston boy?" Although the inmate had already noticed the full size, side-by-side refrigerator-freezer in the small kitchenette to the right of the room, it was the draw of the possibility of the easy escape that made him head to the sliding glass door before considering his hunger. As predicted, the inmate crawled to the refrigerator and pulled himself upright using its door handles. Inside, on the top shelf of the refrigerator was a single item — a white plastic cup with lettering that read: I Love Boston, with a red heart replacing the word Love. The inmate retrieved the cup and looked inside. It was cool to the touch but completely empty. He closed the refrigerator door and gently moved to the small stainless-steel sink positioned just next it. He turned on the right cold-water faucet, but nothing came out of the tap. Next, he turned on the left hot water tap and, for a moment nothing came from it either, until that is, Jack activated the valve that released one-half cup of tepid water. The inmate sat on the couch and tentatively sipped tepid water from the plastic I Love Boston cup as he watched the not-so-breaking news of the Boston bombing.

*IT IS unknown if he knew he ran over his brother during the shootout. As he took off in the stolen Mercedes, the body of the apparent mastermind of the bombing could be seen being dragged for many yards, clothing apparently caught somewhere in the vehicle's suspension. Autopsy reports indicate that, yes indeed, the student killed his own older brother. Speaking through a translator, the mother of the Boston bombers refused to believe her children were involved with any of these horrific events, let alone that one son killed the other.*

THE INMATE WATCHED the rehashed news calmly yet intently despite the fact that none of this was actually new to him. It was just the other day when he again heard the moment-by-moment description his brother's death as retold by the police officers on duty that night as well as what he thought were the pitiful sob stories from some of the survivors of the bombing.

Jack, with a clear front view of the boy's face and body language, knew it was time for another seamless segues into one of many pre-prepared "Breaking News" segments.

*FOR THE FIRST time since their son was moved to a maximum security prison, the parents have granted an interview with their local televi-*

sion station and we will join that interview just as soon as we receive the feed.

It was the first time Jack heard the inmate's voice, and Jack heard him clearly. His strong words were aimed directly at the two-way television screen. "Mama!"

Let us now go live to what...what appears to be startling developments at the interview with the parents of the Boston bombers that are taking place live halfway around the world...and apparently ... oh my...I'm being told that viewer discretion is highly recommended as we watch live the scenes of what has now become...oh my God! During an on-camera interview to discuss the sentencing and imprisonment of their son, a man yielding what appear to be two large hunting knives has attacked the parents of the Boston bombers from the back. As the husband and wife were seated for the interview, the killer could be seen approaching from behind and with great force plunged the knives, one held in each hand, directly in the center of the heads of the...oh my...

Jack clearly heard the guttural sounds of the inmate's spasmodic retching as the camera in the small, unbreakable two-way mirror positioned above the small sink and toilet unit in the cement cell recorded the head of the inmate plunge downward. Amid the heaves, that produced a little water but plenty of acrid bile, were cries of disbelief and confusion. "Mama. No Mama, no," he wailed. "Papa. Mama. What have they done?" Although his strength had been instantly sapped, the young inmate rose unsteadily to his feet and returned to the spacious room where he found the television that, just a moment ago, showed in vivid color the gruesome murder of his parents, was now black. It was off. The young man looked around the room for the remote control but found none. He then ran his hands around the sides and bottom of the television for buttons but found none. Depleted, shocked, and swimming in anguish, he curled up on the couch. Quickly, the former student lapsed into a deep sleep facing the wall-mounted, button-less television.

Jack set the timer on his watch for five minutes.

∼

THE POLICE CAR siren was so piercingly loud, yet so brief, that the only evidence of its occurrence was the result of the instantly released adrenalin that raced through the inmate's once resting body. The inmate leapt from the couch with his heart pounding in the fight-or-flight response of survival. But after a few moments, the young convict gathered himself and he made his way to the refrigerator, again mostly as a teenager-type reflex. To his disbelief, on the once-empty top shelf, was an unopened bag of corn chips. Without a thought on how it made its way to the refrigerator, he retrieved the 14-ounce bag and returned to the couch where he sat to face the television that had just turned on.

*WE NOW CONTINUE our weeklong coverage leading up to the one-year anniversary of the Boston marathon bombing by interviewing one of the surgeons on duty that horrific afternoon. Doctor, would you explain to our viewing audience how a shrapnel injury differs from a typical injury one may experience, say with a knife or a gun?*

*Why, yes of course. Compared with tissue damage from a knife, which can be quite clean with well-delineated edges, the damage caused by shrapnel, and some types of ammunition, is usually quite extensive with edges that are shredded, torn. The tissue is usually destroyed. It is beyond repair. Those nearest the explosions lost entire appendages and surrounding tissues were peppered with fragments of embedded metal. Some of these pieces of sharp metal punctured arteries and veins that resulted in a great deal of blood loss as well as loss of tissue viability. In one patient I removed shrapnel from every organ except the heart. I never saw anything like it before.*

*How long were you operating that day?*

*There were so many victims that everyone just stayed all night and into the next day. Everyone. Pre-Op staff, post-Op staff, nurses, anesthetists, everyone stayed; many came in on their day off to help out. We found ourselves in a race against time with so many patients...it was war-like carnage. It was pure and simple destruction of human tissues, organs, limb and lives. All I did was to try to repair as much as I could, to save as much as I could and to stitch back together the broken pieces. To this day, I don't feel as though I did enough.*

*We only have time for one more question. What was the most enduring image from that day? What will you never forget?*

*There was one person... it was her skin. Despite all of the blood and tissue and things I've seen, I'll never forget her skin. She must have been close to the blast because not only did she lose both of her legs, but the heat from the explosion singed and charred her skin. Most of the charred skin was black, but there were other parts, well they weren't black they were pale, skin colored, and so brittle that these little pieces snapped off like chips. They looked like corn chips dotted with stubs of burned hair. For some odd reason, I'll never forget these strange pieces of skin. I won't eat chips again.*


IT DIDN'T TAKE LONG for the college student-turned-terrorist to put two and two together. Up to this point, he was eating hand-to-mouth with as much enthusiasm as a toddler in a highchair with a tray full of Cheerios. And until this point in time, the young inmate hadn't thought twice about what he was devouring. It wasn't only the third to last chip in the bag that was oddly shaped but all three had various amounts of what could only be hair follicles except that the tops of each short strand of hair didn't end in a tiny point but in a little black ball like a microscopic lollipop that had been dipped in tar.

Unlike his first vomit session, this round of violent upheavals were decisively more productive. Chunks of chips that again found their way pass his taste buds were still both sweet and salty, and remarkably, they still contained tiny bits of singed hair. Dizzy and exhausted, the tough, young inmate lay on the concrete slab that served as his bed in the inner room. While he could still hear the non-stop voices from the wall-mounted television in the room beyond the steel bars, at least he couldn't see the images.

Jack turned up the speaker volume in the cement cell by a few decibels. He didn't want the weary inmate to miss any news that might break at any time, but the increased volume did not stop the inmate from falling asleep. His mind and his body were reeling not only from a difficult year but also from a trying morning. The damaging electric shock was the least of it. His mind could not comprehend the vicious murder of his parents, and although he cared less for his father, he did love his mother deeply. Two questions formed in his subconscious as he drifted off to a mid-morning sleep: Is she really dead? Is anyone really dead?

---

THIS WON'T PROVE ANYTHING. *Even if we are successful, even if we pull this off as you've planned, it won't prove anything. There is no doubt in my mind little brother that this will send a strong message to everyone who doesn't believe in what we believe in. It will make them* see that their capitalistic and self-righteous ways, and the ways of their evil government, a government that they support with their blood tax money, has killed our families; they are trying to destroy our future and all that we've ever believed in. Our message will be loud. It will be clear. And it will be seen for generations as the single point in time when America fell to its knees and begged for forgiveness. America is already a failing country and our role is to make sure it goes down forever. The American way, Satan's way, will be destroyed. Totally destroyed.

But we are young. We will die in the process. Can we not carry out our crusade in a different way? We will kill and be killed. Then we will be useless.

Must I say it again? You must trust me. I've learned a great deal from watching videos. They all were reckless. They were amateurs. That's why they were killed. We have been in this pathetic country for over a decade, we know how stupid and sloppy these American people are, that's why not one of them is my friend, I have nothing in common with these people. They are too stupid.

But you married an American!

Do you not think she is part of the ruse? She's a toy, a decoy as I told you before. The plan, including our escape is simple. All of the parts are already in place and these idiots don't even know it. Look at this map. We will hail a taxi here. We place our backpacks in the trunk and have a ride to here. We then walk here, turn here, me first; we will not be together from this point until we reunite later here. I will leave my backpack here, and you will leave yours here. Once you do drop it off, start counting and walking. No running, it will draw attention. When your count reaches sixty, after you turn the corner here, I will detonate both of them and meet you at this corner right here where we will get another cab.

And then what should I do?

What would you normally do?

Go back to school. I have classes the next day.

*Then go back to school. You're done. We're done. We've done our job. And after everything calms down, we'll do it again someday, probably in another city. Actually, I may go to New Hampshire and go on a hike. But you should go back to school. Be with your friends and watch the beauty of it all.*

*What if they ask where I've been?*

*Who?*

*My friends. What if this actually works and there is news coverage and my friends ask me if I was near the explosion, what should I say?*

*What would you normally say?*

*I'd just say that I went to see you in Cambridge this weekend and we were just hanging out.*

*Then just say that. Offer nothing.*

*And what if something goes wrong?*

*Like what?*

*Like the bombs explode in the back of the cab or when we're carrying them or something. What if we die either in the process or afterwards?*

*Then we will die as martyrs. Those that understand what we were trying to do will know. They will resurrect us and revere our images for all time. We will live in glory in the next world.*

*And those we injure or kill?*

*They deserve no mercy. No pity. Nothing. I hate them. I hate all Americans. They are not like us. Our cause is righteous, and their ways are Satan's ways.*


THE WORD SATAN reverberated in the inmate's mind. It rekindled a childhood image of the evil one – a masterful blend of a narrow, red-faced person with sharp vampire-like teeth, sharp white horns perched on the top of his head, piercing green eyes that saw directly to your soul, pointed ears and a V-shaped goatee – that had been the cause of vivid nightmares by the inmate in his youth. He woke with a gasp of fright and with a racing heart. Everything was near dark. The cement cell was black, as was the outer room. The television was off. And a low wattage night-light illuminated the bottom half of the refrigerator. Thirst, hunger, confusion and disorientation were combined with localized pain on his side from having slept on the slab of cement. He thought about trying the shower but instead of taking the few steps to the corner of the cement cell, the young inmate walked towards the light and once again opened the refrigerator door. Through the blinding bright light was a brown paper bag. The inmate felt the cold air fall onto his bare feet as he looked inside the bag to see a small sub, a can of soda, and a small bag of chips. He removed the sandwich and soda but kept the chips in the bag. He drank half the can of soda before he walked the short distance to the soft leather sofa. Coincident with his sitting down on the sofa, the recessed lights in the kitchen turned on.

"There you are little boy. See your dinner now?" Jack said with eyes glued to the monitor. "Perhaps you need more light to better inspect your sandwich? Don't you want to see what you're eating?" It was as if the inmate heard Jack's questions. Just before he bit the sandwich he peeled back and inspected each slice of cold cut for signs of hair. There wasn't any, so he put the sandwich back together and ate it. The boy inmate stared at the blank television screen as if it would turn on by that simple action. But this evening there would be no breaking news. Jack had other plans.

"Time to brush up on your history," Jack said aloud as he activated a switch from the control room. The television's background remained black as words in bold, white lettering began to scroll upwards from the bottom of the screen. For the next hour, the convicted boy terrorist was treated to a chronicle of intimidation against individuals or groups or entire populations residing in the United States of America. The silent words spanned the actions and outcomes of over 200 years of violence. The brutal actions of organized small groups or the wayward person in the name of perceived justice, religion, race, individual rights, or one of several other causes that suited the perpetrator or perpetrators. The inventory read like the Who's Who of Vehemence. Names, ages, motivations and ultimate fate of the leaders of all groups that attacked the homeland were also included.

The sentenced-to-death child terrorist was attentive throughout the entire presentation. His did not fidget nor stray from his position in front of the silent monitor. But as the chronologically presented information approached the date when the child terrorist committed his own acts, his name as well as that of his mastermind brother was conspicuously absent. The timeline simply moved along as if his fifteen minutes of fame had never happened at all. And when it reached present day, the screen went total black along with the entire room. It was as if there had been no more history to disclose. No updates. No shootings. No more terror to report.

Had the Earth stopped rotating?

All was calm on this silent night. Not even the waxing gibbous moon that would rise in a few more hours was present to provide a shred of light to the two-chambered cell. All was quiet. It was just black. And with nothing else to do the child terrorist lay on his right side on the soft, black leather sofa. He needed to think. He was beginning to question the events of the past year. Did they really happen or is this all a bad dream? Wasn't he just a student learning about things in college? And what if all of this was true? What would transpire during his remaining time? Has he really been sentenced to death? What did it mean to die? Rather, what did it mean to live, anyway?

In no time, he was again sound asleep, but even if he had

been awake, he would have not heard the large needle pierce the thin foam-plaster ceiling directly above his head. A single green laser beam ensured that the opening of the needle was positioned such that the contents of the attached plastic cylinder would land within a three-inch square area near the sleeping terrorist's temple.

Jack watched the special monitor connected to the tiny infrared camera located within the wall-mounted television. The extreme close-up of the inmate's head with a new growth of hair was on its side and in repose when the small rubber plug bounced softly off of his temple. Neither the small plug nor the first four drops of pig's blood were felt by the sleeping inmate, but the fifth drop made his entire body shift slightly. Despite the movement of the child-terrorist Jack did not need to adjust the position of the needle. Drop by drop by drop by drop warm blood continued to land on the inmate's head until a small trickle made its way in front of the boy's ear and onto the leather sofa. Jack counted. Eleven, twelve, thirteen, fourteen, fifteen drops made their way from the inmate's face onto the leather couch before the boy inmate wiped the liquid sleepily with his left hand, which then drooped and hung, bloodied, off the front of the sofa.

With a push of a button Jack activated the strobe lights. From the back wall of the kitchen came momentary bursts of blinding white light. The bursts came regularly every three seconds for a full minute, then every second for the next five minutes. Flash, flash, flash. Drip, drip, drip. Flash, drip, flash, drip, flash, drip, flash, drip, flash, drip. Jack watched intently as the inmate stirred and repositioned himself onto his back such that now the pig's blood landed on the upper lip of the partially sleeping inmate. Increased pulses of brilliant white light meant that the infrared camera was no longer needed; the room was most almost fully lit.

The inmate's eyes blinked open. He sat straight up when he realized that he had just wiped sticky warm blood off his face. Flashes of a second strobe light, this one red, started in rapid bursts from a second location in the kitchen along with silent but brightly colored, high-resolution images that appeared in rapid-fire on the television. Images of blood splattered store windows, fire hydrants, mailboxes, signs, clothing, granite curbs, on the pavement itself in trickles or on the side walk in small pools and in large pools, and on the clothes of people who didn't know they were in shock, on running shoes, so many running shoes, on emergency gurneys, on hands, feet, heads, knees, hair, racing bibs, handbags, trash cans, faces, lots of faces. Bright red blood was even splattered on the little round, panicked face of a little baby seated in stroller, crying mutedly, and waving wildly in the air the shredded remains of her pudgy, little right hand; the intensity of the pain foreign to her.

Flash-flash red, flash-flash white, drip-drip-drip.

The inmate's head ratcheted from side-to-side as if the strobe lights controlled his movements. He half-ran from the bloodstained room to the far corner of the dark cement cell where he removed his blood-soaked clothes, sat on the cement floor and cried loudly and forcefully. He wished with all of his might that the water would cleanse him of his blood and of his great sin. But Jack wasn't ready to turn on the water just yet. Instead, he unmuted the sounds that accompanied the images on the television and now, seated on top of the small floor drain in a crouched position in the dry shower, the man-boy terrorist heard the sounds of terror, the sounds of pain, the sounds of anguish, the sounds of disbelief, the sounds of chaos, and the piercing shriek of a baby. They were the sounds that resulted from the actions of a twisted, sordid, unsound mind – a mind he now knew so well. He covered his ears in an attempt to dampen the damning audio display of terror, a move that made Jack increase the volume of the full-range speakers embedded in the walls of the cement cell. Distinct sounds of human suffering filled the room as ice cold water suddenly gushed from the ceiling-encased nozzle. Wails from the inmate mixed with the sounds that originated from the television as Jack watched the now diluted pig's blood swirl down the small floor drain.

*Two years ago today we were standing right here on this very spot, in Hopkinton, Massachusetts at the start of the Boston marathon; the skies were deep blue as they are today, and electricity was in the air then as it is now. Two years ago, no one thought the word terrorism would be in the same sentence with the Boston marathon, but this year, like last year is different. Or is it? To answer this question, I'm joined by a young lady who has run this race each year for the past ten years and I'd like to thank you for joining me this morning. I know you have a lot on your mind.*

*Well, thank you for the opportunity to let my family and friends know that I'm running this today for them and for all of the volunteers that worked the marathon year in and year out.*

*Do you have any safety concerns about today's race?*

*No, none at all. Two years ago, I was not allowed to finish and last year I wasn't ready mentally. But this year I've doubled my training efforts, and I'm ready to go. I've also raised a great deal of money for the victims and their families so I'm excited to get going.*

*Good over evil, would you agree?*

*Absolutely. And as a bonus I won a lottery for a free pair of running sneakers. I've never heard of this brand, but 101 pairs were raffled off three months ago; an anonymous person donated these sneakers as an example of good will. They're awesome!*

*Well, good luck to you today and thank you for taking the time to speak with us. Good luck.*

. . .

THE HARD SLAB in the cement room was not a place to take comfort, but it was where the boy inmate spent most of his time because it is where he felt safe. He feared the light of day as much as he did the blackness of night. The luxurious living space with the kitchen, refrigerator, wall-mounted television and black leather sofa outside of the cement cell that was once a viewed as a type of wonderland was now where dangers lurked. How things came and went in the living space outside of the cement room was a complete mystery, but appear and disappear they did.

Bags of food as well as cold water in plastic containers that dissolved into a slimy puddle as they warmed to room temperature, were often left in the refrigerator. And sometimes other items, such as the bloodied stump of a child's foot, a kneecap with gangrenous cartilage tissue had also been placed in the cold chamber alongside non-GMO edibles. Once there was even an unblinking eyeball nestled snugly in the plastic container that was intended for eggs. These and other items simply appeared one day only to disappear some time later. There was no rhyme or reason to what might be found outside the confines of the cement cell on any given day.

The boy terrorist lay on his left side on the cement slab and faced the cement wall. Other than the glow that emitted from the large wall mounted television on the room outside the cement room, there was no light. Based on the news feed it was a Monday in April, the day of the marathon in Boston.

"Welcome to your two-year anniversary," Jack said to the monitor that showed the boy inmate. "There are presents for you. Come on out and have a look. I'm sure you'll recognize them."

One pressure cooker was in plain view and it looked quite natural on top of the stove while the other was hidden inside a black backpack by the sliding glass door. Both were identical in size and shape but only the one on the floor made a sound. The ticking sound that emanated from the pressure cooker in the backpack on the floor were not as rapid as those of a stopwatch nor were they as slow as those of a grandfather's clock, indeed they altogether differed – they were irregular. Tick-tick-tick-tick-silence-silence-tick-silence-tick-tick-silence-tick-silence-silence-silence...

These unusual sounds make the convict leave his cement bed and walk out into the room outside the cell. His heart raced when he saw the shiny pressure cooker on top the stove. He immediately and mistakenly assumed that the ticking sounds came from that once respected cookware. Cautiously and ever so tentatively he walked to it. He planned to simply pick up the entire thing and throw straight through the sliding glass doors. But as the child terrorist approached the stove, he spotted the black bag near the sliding glass door. It was a bag that looked familiar. Indeed, it was identical to one he carried to the marathon two years ago. The inmate's pulse spiked to new heights for it was from within that very bag where the erratically spaced ticks emanated. The convict went to the bag by the sliding glass door and gently peered inside. Weld joints could be seen on the seam of the pressure cooker inside the bag. Tick-tick-silence-silence-silence-tick-tick came from inside the cooker. Just then the magnetic burner directly underneath the pressure cooker on the stove began to glow red.

Jack watched intently as the pressure cooker on the stove, also with its seams welded, shot sparkler-type sparks from the release valve perched on the top cover. The bright white sparks along with the sizzling sounds caused the inmate to scream out loud. He then retreated to the narrow space underneath the slab of the cement cell where he awaited the pending explosion.

But there would be no explosion, at least not in Cell X. The sounds he heard came from the speakers. The television repeatedly showed the explosions that occurred two years ago by homemade bombs made by the boy terrorist and his older, now long dead brother. The blasts occurred over and over and over as the sounds echoed louder and louder and louder through the speakers placed throughout the two-chambered cell. The sounds of the first blast seemed so real that the boy under the slab braced his thin body by bringing his knees up close to his chest as he turned towards the wall to protect his face. The overall feeling of dread he felt was reminiscent of the time spent underneath a tarp in a boat perched on land somewhere. He thought now the same thoughts he thought then: *My end is near.*

UNBEKNOWNST to the prisoner in hiding was that the humidity of the entire area of Cell X was slowly increasing such that when he eventually moved out from underneath the cement slab, he found himself shrouded in cloud of dense fog. The sounds of the bombs in his cell as well as those on the television were silenced. The looped footage of the dual explosions stopped. Instead, the television showed what appeared to be a live feed from the present day's Boston marathon.

*JUST LOOK at this sea of humanity stretching for miles as every one of these remarkable runners makes their personal journey to Boston. Many run to raise money for those battling diseases, or the memory of a lost loved one, and many running this race as a tribute to those affected by the events of two years ago. And then there are those remarkable athletes that have lost legs now running with specially fitted prosthetics, running blades, as they are called. Remarkable technology and remarkable people behind that technology, many that make Boston and the surrounding suburbs their workplace and home. Speaking of technology, we learned just about an hour ago that the*

*101 pairs of sneakers given freely by an anonymous donor to runners that qualified for today's event will monitor and transmit in real-time, metrics, otherwise known as data, on the health of the runner. As the wearer of these high-tech sneakers pass underneath an overhead receiver that look like those toll collectors on the interstate highway, data from the transmitter embedded in these sneakers will record the actual mile pace of the runner, as well as the runner's heart rate, body temperature, and blood pressure. Remarkable. There are four of these overhead receivers at the 5, 10, 15-mile marks and the last one at the finish line. Truly remarkable.*

AT FIRST THE inmate felt only a couple. Then he felt a few more. Then he felt nothing for a moment or two. A short while later, the unmistakable tingling sensation was felt over the surface of his entire body, although now they came not as singular pulses but as erratic, rapid fire beats like raindrops striking a metal roof during a downpour. The odd sensations made him squirm to his feet. The boy terrorist looked around the fog-filled room looking for something that might explain the strange sensations he felt. He had no idea. Indeed no one did, no one, that is, except for Jack.

From the control room Jack watched not only the child terrorist in Cell X and the defeated rapist in Cell Z but also a real-time video feed of the runners in Boston that were crossing the 5-mile mark. Alongside the monitor labeled "Boston5K" was a computer display of scrolling data transmitted from each of the 101 pairs of sneakers.

The first use of the new technology was working flawlessly.

"Now wasn't that thoughtful?" Jack said aloud to the multi-phased monitor that showed the child terrorist in different spectra, including infrared. "Those nice runners in Boston each sent you two little half-milliamp pokes, one from each sneaker. Tickles, don't it? If you liked that little bit of attention, then sit back and relax, you're going to really enjoy the next one." Jack had to wait a little over thirty minutes to watch how the inmate and his conductive thin body reacted to pulses of one milliamp current. The boy terrorist sat on the floor in front of the leather sofa and watched the muted television when the first two shocks arrived in rapid succession. Again, he looked around the misty room but he saw little and the only thing he heard was the tick-tick-tick-silence-silence-tick-tick that once again came from inside the bag by the sliding glass door. Before he had a chance to check on the pressure cooker on the stove, he felt yet more shocks. This time the pulses felt more like small hail striking a tin roof, they were more pronounced. A short period of time later, the hailstorm arrived with a vengeance, yet the inmate made no connection to events that unfolded on television and what he was experiencing physically.

"How about five little milliamps, hmm?" Jack asked the monitor.

Marathoners realize that they're on the home stretch when they cross the 15-mile mark. For many participants, including those fortunate enough to receive a free pair of sneakers, running suddenly becomes more enjoyable when pleasure hormones called endorphins are released. That when the rugged ordeal has become nothing but enjoyable. The crowds near the finish line are enthusiastic, the cheers and shouts of encouragement become louder, and now the finish line is not a pipe dream but just a matter of time.

For the boy terrorist, however, the 15-mile mark was outright painful. Out were the raindrops and hail and in were sharp stones – piercing shocks. Random muscles on the lean boy inmate's body contracted at will, movements that made him look more like a poorly constructed wooden puppet then it did a functioning human being. He thrashed around the outer room so violently that he tried desperately, and somewhat successfully, to guide himself to the softness of the leather sofa in an effort to limit the damaging effects of the shocks. Tick-tick-silence-tick-tick-tick-tick was what he heard, dense fog is what he saw, and piercing pain is what he felt – seemingly endless jolts of piercing pain.

The inmate's writhing and screams didn't faze Jack in the least.

It was Matthew 5:38 that was Jack's guiding light. That simple bible verse and the faces of infants and children and adults of all ages, of all sects, of all colors, from all lands whose lives had been destroyed by those like the boy terrorist who held no remorse for their inhumane actions that covered the walls of the control room. Jack knew full well that the torments endured by those that entered Cell X, or Cell Y or Cell Z would not undo what had been done, would not heal the wounds or bring back the dead. He knew that hate never had an equal opposite, but he did know that hate would endure. He knew that somewhere in the tightly compacted chromosomes of all humans were genes ready to explode in violence, ready to rape, destroy, murder, cause chaos, but he also knew that those that do not learn the errors of their ways, do not understand right from wrong, yes from no, black from white, were destined to pass along their ill intent, and Jack had had enough of it. He would see to it that those that entered Cell X, Cell Y or Cell Z were not going to have the chance to pass along their genes to anyone. Sometimes things have to end.

BY NIGHTFALL IN BOSTON, after all the marathon runners had safely crossed the finish line, and after the boy terrorist was zapped with 202-10 amps jolts, did the tick-tick-ticking stop and the cloud in the room dissipate. The television was off. All rooms in Cell X were pitch black and still. In the far corner of the cement cell, visible by infrared camera only, the convict lay shivering and weakly whimpering in a tight fetal position. The convicted boy terrorist, burned in various spots was reduced for at least this one life sentence to a pathetic shell of a human being, one who would forever curse those who apprehended him alive.

⁓

JACK LEANED back in his comfortable black leather office chair and glanced at the video images of the broken men-boy murders that lay alone: one quietly in Cell X and the other in Cell Z. His gaze left the monitors, moved upward and to the right to a wall covered with hundreds of photographs of those who had fallen victim by the unnecessary violence perpetrated by the men whom have passed through his facility over the years.

It wasn't that Jack simply stared at the faces of the little boy with the dimpled chin and red hair, or the middle-aged man dressed sharply in his fireman blues, or the elderly lady with silver gray hair with small eyes and a forced smile, it wasn't that Jack just looked at these photographs of dead people, but each and every one spoke to him. Very few elaborated on the tragedy that killed them, but all spoke with passion about what might have been. At the end they all asked the same question: Why?

The little boy with the red hair said that he missed his puppy and his bed and his Superman toothbrush. He told Jack that the policeman held him tight and told him that everything was going to be okay but then he died. He asked why he died and if he would be alive again someday. He also asked Jack if a kid dying was normal.

The firefighter said that he handed a little boy off to a policeman who looked shocked to see the rapidly beating little heart through the cracked open wound in the child's sternum. He remembered that he went back in the bombed building because there were more people to help. How was he to know that the metal rafter above would crush his head despite his protective helmet as if both were composed of paper mâché? He thought it was quite funny that he didn't even know he was dead. The affable first responder said with a chuckle that the line between life and death was so razor thin, so transparent, that it didn't really exist at all.

The elderly lady asked incessantly, as if Jack would know, why she insisted on bringing her grandson with her when the child simply wanted to stay home and play chess with his grandfather, her husband. She admitted to being old and deadworthy, but she also lamented the fact that she would forever bear responsibility of the death of her grandson, the little boy with the side of his head missing. To Jack, the elderly lady spoke only about her grandson, and of her decision to bring him with her that fateful day. Once she told him that the family was right to blame her. It was her cross-in-perpetuity to bear.

Towards the bottom of the wall of picture and clippings of new articles of the tragedies was a black and white photograph of another little girl dressed in a pink, frilly fairy outfit. Her little voice was easily rendered in Jack's head, especially when she told him that she would wear a pretty dress like this when she got married. But it wasn't the imagined sound of his little girl's voice, nor the site of her fairy outfit, nor her projected thoughts into a future that would never exist that made Jack weep, it was her innocent questions. In her little girl high-pitched voice, she asked repeatedly: *Will you be there Daddy? Will you dance with me?*

## APPEAL

"Your honor, my client fully acknowledges that he, along with his brother, conceived of and carried out an act of terrorism on unsuspecting, innocent Americans. He is aware of his actions and he would like the United States government to proceed rapidly with fulfilling its duty to put him to death as deemed appropriate by a jury of his peers. He has waved any further appeals and would like to have his death sentenced performed by any means possible, judiciously, and without delay."

The judge winked at the attorney. "Tell your client that there are a lot of people on death row. He'll have to wait his turn."

The attorney nodded and winked back.

EPILOGUE

The little boy was riding his bike on the cement sidewalk one bright, warm summer's morning when he spotted a black ant. Instantly, as if the sight of the little creature tripped a hair-triggered switch, the normally tranquil little boy became enraged. He became as mad as his father was when he yelled and screamed and beat his mother as a part of the daily ritual. He became as fearsome as the school bully who made a girl in his class wet her pants when he threatened to shoot her with his father's handgun if she didn't do what he wanted her to do to him. He mirrored the attitude of those well-dressed, all-knowing people on that cable news station on the big television that was always on who constantly yelled and appeared angry, especially when they spoke about people who didn't look like them or who didn't live in their neighborhood.

The little boy had had enough of those ugly black ants. He hated all of them and it was high time he did something about it. So, he got off his bike, went into the toolshed and found a hammer. He crouched down next to his bike on the sidewalk and waited. When he saw the next one, he did not hesitate. His move was as deliberate and definitive as it was obvious and necessary. The crouching little boy, with eyebrows furled in determination, swung the hammer that struck the ant with so much force that the ant's once internal body parts and fluids caused it to stick to the head of the hammer; in essence, the ant disappeared in mid-air. But the little boy was not fooled. He did not think the ant disappeared at all. He twisted the hammer's handle to reveal the slimy mess on the silver, round face of the hammer's head, and because the ant was no longer bothering him, he left it right where it was.

While he was inspecting the splattered ant on the hammer's head, in the periphery of his vision, he saw another black ant. Quickly, he imagined himself as some kind of a sharp shooter with a lethal weapon, he swung the wooden-handled tool at the unsuspecting ant. However, unlike his first strike, the hammer's rounded head crushed only the lower half of the unsuspecting black ant. The little boy looked at the result of his deed with a curious blend of fantastical wonderment and demonic pleasure. The top half of the ant was alive despite the obliteration of its lower half; its head was moving left to right, as if it was watching traffic flow on a two-way highway at rush hour; it's tiny two front legs flailed aimlessly. For a second, the little boy thought about smacking it again to kill it completely, but he didn't because he couldn't see the point; that black ant couldn't bother him now, it was good and broken. Bored, the child dropped the hammer. He then picked up his bike and rode away thinking that if he saw any more ants he would just run them over. His treasured bike quickly became his new weapon of choice – it was faster and much easier to use. Now he could kill a great number of black ants, or any type of ant, for that matter.

The life in the half-flattened black ant forgotten on the sidewalk was waning rapidly. Although it wasn't sure why it couldn't move the rear end of its segmented little body, it knew with certainty that it was in trouble, and that an important message had to be transmitted to its colony mates. With the release of the right chemical signal, the immobilized ant attracted, and then interacted, with one of its own – each rubbing the other's flexible feelers. The message, which was actually a reinforcing one, was precise. Over the next few weeks, the chemically-encoded directive was passed along to all other members of the underground colony, and to all other ant colonies on the continent regardless of their minor anatomical differences.

For ants, as well as for other highly-structured, social creatures on planet Earth, it's not a matter of fleeting hatred towards humans – it's a matter of lasting revenge.

THE END

# IRRELEVANCE

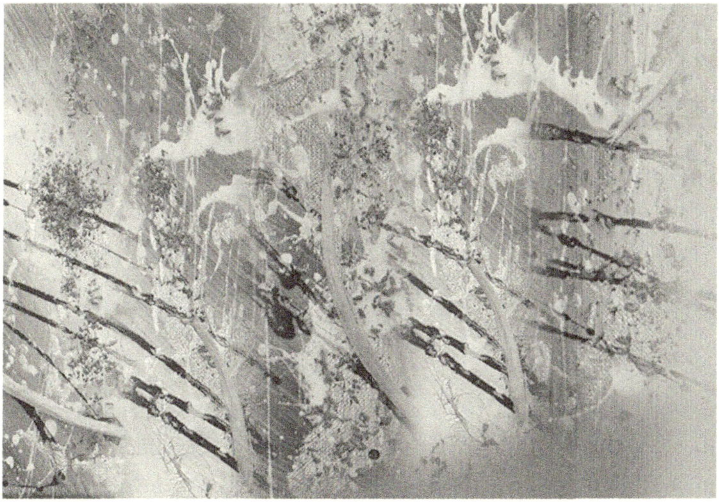

## ROOM K78

All ten students had the same thought: *Is this some kind of joke?*

The new wing of Cathedral Ledge High School had everything a 21st-century structure required. High-speed wireless Internet, solar panels on the roof, thermal-paned, energy-producing windows, and a blend of natural and artificial lighting in each room that adjusted every fifteen minutes by a computer-controlled video camera according to the level of alertness of its occupants. The hallways were coated with high-gloss, scuff and dirt resistant flooring that led not to wide open, glass-walled rooms but to a series of smaller individual rooms that allowed for intimately sized classes of twenty or less. In response to well-controlled research studies on student participation and learning retention, planners sought to shrink, not expand, classroom size.

Yet oddly, the inside of room K78, located off the right side of the futuristic looking hallway, was the polar opposite of modern. The room was a throwback to a time before any of the students were born. It was not even a classroom that their parents would recognize; in fact, the students recalled the stories from their grandparents about blackboards and pull-down maps. Sentences, arithmetic problems and homework assignments were written on the hard surface with pencil-like pieces of white chalk neatly contained in small yellow and green colored boxes that, along with small, brick-shaped felt erasers, were placed on each end of the aluminum trays that ran the entire length of the blackboard. These boards were mounted on the front wall as well as on the walls of each side of the odd, windowless room. Words and numbers written on the blackboard with the little sticks of chalk were then cleared with the felt erasers that were somewhat reconditioned by clapping them together out of doors, a chore that created a white cloud of dust around the unfortunate clapper.

Small wooden desks in the room were more like modified high chairs. They were one-piece metal and wood units with a seat that contained a small back support and a surface for reading and writing. Four rows of five small wooden desks faced the front of the room where a larger, plain rectangular desk that faced the small desks was positioned. A multicolored, pull down map of the world nearly covered the entire back wall of the room.

High on the wall above the door was a plain black clock that indicated that it was almost eight o'clock. The Advanced Mathematics class was scheduled to start in less than thirty-seconds when all ten students had the exact same thought.

It took the second hand sweep of the plain black clock three more tics to reach the number twelve when the door underneath it opened so abruptly, so forcefully and with so much certainty that most of the students seated in their little desks were soundly startled.

The person who walked through the door at precisely eight o'clock in the morning matched the décor of the classroom; he appeared to be from either the 1950s or perhaps even the 1940s.

His shoulders were hunched and he looked as if he was a slightly shrunken version of his former, more youthful, self. His wispy thin hair was pearl white and decidedly in disarray. His black, Browline wayfarer glasses hung heavily on his thick nose. The old man wore a white button-down shirt, a brown patternless tie, a dark-gray vest and a well-worn brown herringbone tweed sports coat. His brown trousers appeared as though they fit him better years ago; the turned-up cuffs mostly hid the worn dark brown leather shoes.

Not a word was spoken as he placed the faded tan leather briefcase on top of the desk at the front of the room. The old man seemed to be in his own world as he silently turned his back to the students, picked up a piece of white chalk and in clear letters wrote on the blackboard:

---

Math and science are relevant. You are not.

---

He then turned and faced the dumbstruck students. His eyebrows knitted slightly as if he was trying to bring each young face into sharp focus. A full two minutes passed before he asked in a forceful, gruff voice, "Questions?"

Each of the ten students shifted uncomfortably in their hard, wooden seat. Someone had to say something but given that the entire scene – from the old fashion classroom to the crusty old man to the odd statement he wrote on the blackboard – was so bizarre, everyone was frozen silent. Finally, a young lady seated at the first desk of the second row raise her hand ever so tentatively. The old man's head turned sharply to face the petite brunette.

"Speak!" he commanded.

"I don't understand what you wrote," the sixteen-year-old student said meekly.

"Read it out loud," the old man demanded. The young brunette did as she was told.

"Do you understand it now?" he asked.

"No, not really."

"Then read it again and stop after every word."

"Math," she said.

"Does everyone understand the meaning of that word?" he asked the class. Everyone nodded.

"Are you sure?" Again, everyone nodded.

"Continue," he said to the brunette.

"And science."

"Stop! Does everyone understand what is meant by 'science'?" Again, everyone nodded as though they all knew the meaning of the word. But the old man was not convinced.

"You, you with the curly hair. How old are you?" the old man asked the young man who sat to the brunette's left.

"I...I just turned...seventeen," the curly haired boy stammered.

"Well, mister seventeen-year-old, since you nodded your head, tell all of us what does the word 'science' mean?"

"S-s-science is the st-study of, you know, things like nature and th-things."

"Just as I thought," sighed the old man as he walked behind the desk. He proceeded to pull out the wooden desk chair and sat in it. "Just as I thought."

The plump strawberry blonde girl seated behind the stammering seventeen-year-old came to her classmate's rescue. "It's more like learning and appreciating our natural and physical world through experimentation and observation. There are many different branches of science such as biology, physics, astronomy and chemistry."

"That's more like it. Continue reading."

The plump strawberry blonde girl did as she was told.

"Are relevant," she said before she automatically stopped at the semi-colon.

"Does anyone want to take a stab at the meaning of 'relevant'?"

"It's being real," offered the curly haired boy in an effort to improve on his earlier answer. The old man turned away from the obviously flawed answer and looked to his left at the freckled redhead boy seated in the first seat of the fourth row. He locked eyes with the thin-faced teenager until he volunteered a response.

"If you are 'relevant' then you're important, needed. You're like key, needed for whatever it is that's happening. It's like you're significant."

"Finish the sentence," the old man commanded of the freckled face redhead. And the student did as he was told.

"Anyone?" challenged the white-haired old man who was starting to sound angry, as if he was losing patience.

The teenager seated in the second desk of the third row was the largest of all of his fellow classmates. Judging from the black tight-fitting shirt with a well-recognized logo displayed across his wide chest, the teenager was an athlete. His strong build made the confines of the desk very uncomfortable, and he seemed to be losing patience with the charade promoted by the old man.

"What you wrote on the board doesn't make sense," said the athlete in a deep, solidly firm voice. "How can topics like math and science be important but we're not? Without us, there would be no math or science or anything for that matter."

The old man rose swiftly and in a flash was leaning over the empty desk positioned in front of the deep-voiced athlete.

"Are you implying that 'important' is the same as 'relevant'?

Is that what I heard? Do you see the word 'important' on the board?" the old man growled at the athlete. The athlete exhaled sharply and broke away from the old man's glare. He wasn't sure if the two words were synonyms or if they meant different things depending on context; all he knew was that the old man did not look pleased.

The old man stood his ground and continued to address the athlete. "Let's assume for a moment that I wrote 'important' instead of 'relevant'. Let's pretend that the two words are synonyms, that they could be used interchangeably. Now then, how old are you?"

"I'll be nineteen soon," replied the athlete who again shifted in the tight desk.

"How soon?"

The athlete knew he had been had. "Eleven months."

"I thought so," replied the old man.

"And are you 'important' or 'relevant'? Choose one."

"Obviously, I'm both," the athlete said with a smirk. But when the athlete peered at those seated around him, he realized that no one else was sharing in his moment of lightheartedness. The small desk suddenly seemed tighter.

The old man was all business. "I said, choose one."

"All right then, I'll pick 'important'. I'm important."

"Why?"

"Because I'm the quarterback of the football team, that's why."

Seated to the right of the athlete was a petite Asian woman with ink-black hair that was neatly pulled back into a ponytail. Her hands were folded on top of the desk that for her was perfectly sized. The old man turned to her and asked, "The quarterback here thinks he's important. Is he important?"

The Asian student knew that the old man was asking a rhetorical question. He was asking her something deeper, something greater than her opinion of the athlete's prominence. She glanced quickly at the blackboard then back at the old man.

"He is neither important nor relevant, just as math and science are neither important nor relevant." Her sharply delivered sentence was followed by a roomful of silence, a response that morphed into low-level murmurs that rapidly rippled across the small room. Her classmates were stunned by her bold reply. With one sentence it seemed she insulted the athlete, ended the old man's line of wayward questioning, and dismissed altogether the statement written on the blackboard.

The old man turned to his right and walked slowly towards the wall opposite the door, a place that contained windows in other classrooms. He then pivoted again to his right so that he again faced the blackboard, his back to the students. "Is she correct? Two topics, one person. Irrelevant? Unimportant? I'm asking you, young lady, who is sitting directly behind the person who just spoke. I assume you two are friends?"

"Um, yes. Why, yes, we are friends, in fact," replied the tall, natural blonde who was surprised that the old man correctly knew of the relationship with her classmate. The two met when the Asian woman transferred to Cathedral Ledge High School two years prior. They became instant friends because they both shared a deep love of art and philosophy. "And, yes. She is right. Clearly, she is right."

The old man again startled the class with his booming voice. "Why in the world would these two young ladies who are no older than eighteen years of age consider a living, breathing person devoid of importance, as well as declaring him to be completely relevant? And why would they apply the same sentence on mere subjects of study? Why?" He spun on his heels and walked a few steps down rows one and two, between the curly haired stutterer and the petite brunette. "Why?"

There were only three students who had yet to speak a word,

and the old man looked at each of them in succession. The boy with thick glasses, who appeared to be no older than twelve, looked as though he was going to breakdown and cry if called upon. All he did was look straight ahead at the back of the petite brunette's head while trying mightily, and in vain, to become invisible. Two young ladies, both dark-skinned and tight lipped, diagonally flanked the young-looking boy with thick glasses to the rear. Whether by design or by accident, the dark-skinned young lady seated in row one, desk three close to the wall that would have contained windows, formulated a response in her mind; a response that was easily transmitted to the old man by her beautiful brown eyes, eyes that the old man locked onto tightly.

Knowing that she had something to say, the dark-skinned young lady with the beautiful brown eyes quickly rearranged words in her head then deleted most of them to simplify her answer, "They lack context."

The old man stood his position and waited for the student to qualify her response. She knew exactly what the old man was striving to extract from the class. It was an answer that the two female friends on the opposite side of the room knew as well. So confident was the dark-skinned young lady with the beautiful brown eyes of her answer that she stood up from her one-piece desk. She stood tall with her shoulders back, her round chin slightly elevated. She turned slightly to face the old man then she repeated and expanded her answer. "They lack context. My classmate is, as we all are, not important. Nor are we relevant, just as you have written on the board. On the field of competitive play, the skill of the individual athlete to the success of the team is of obvious importance. He is also relevant to the ramifications of the team's success or failure outside the field of play. In those situations, and in similar situations, the individual is both important and relevant. Mathematics, the sciences, physics and all other fields of study can be considered relevant and quite necessary but only when they are applied. Only then can others comprehend their importance. Without individuals to apply these subjects, they too are meaningless. In essence, even the simplest molecule that lacks a neighbor, a positive without a negative, lacks structure or purpose."

The old man made his way back to the desk in the front of the room and, for the first time, sat in the wide wooden chair. Now he conclusively knew who among the ten students were shallow thinkers and who among them thought deeply; as expected half of the class harbored no ability to think at all. With closed eyes and hands folded on the top of the wooden desk the old man seemed pensive, and it appeared as though he was about to say a prayer or to take a nap. And as if they feared acting any other way, the ten students were in a state of attentive obedience. Only one, the athlete, fidgeted, but he did so silently.

∽

WITHOUT OPENING HIS EYES, the old man spoke directly to the petite brunette seated directly in front of him. He chose the young lady not because she was a deep thinker or a shallow thinker, but precisely because she was only an average thinker. She was a bold yet self-assured average thinker.

"You," he said pointing to the petite brunette her with the index finger of his right hand, "what is your career choice?"

Without hesitation the young woman answered. "I'd like to be a veterinarian. I love animals."

"Animals," replied the old man. "Animals are necessary for the survival of humans. The domestication of animals, of man's ability to control their reproduction in order to nourish early versions of our species, led to increased intellect through larger brains; a consistent source of nutrients complemented by the farming of plants. Without them we would not have made it this far. Would you not agree?"

"I meant pets. Animals that are pets," replied the petite brunette.

"Do you consider animals that are pets relevant?"

"Yes. They make people happy and that's important."

"More relevant than animals that are raised for food?"

"Definitely. I think all animals should be free."

"I see. But pets aren't free, now are they?"

"Yes, they are. They are free and they make people live better lives."

The old man looked at the curly haired young man seated to the petite brunette's left and asked, "Is she right? Do pets make people live better lives?"

"I-I guess," he stammered.

"Do you have pets?"

"N-no, I don't."

"Why?"

"A-a-allergies. I'm a-allergic to cats and d-dogs," replied the curly haired young man who, due to his speech impediment, preferred to simply listen. The old man turned to the young lady who wanted to be a pet veterinarian. "So, would you say that pets are important to him?" he asked pointing to the curly haired young man.

"Perhaps not today but someday they will be," said the petite brunette with conviction.

The old man's eyebrows knitted together for a brief moment as if they were trying to deflect the path of an incoming fly. And ignoring the obvious discomfort of the curly haired teenager, the old man asked him the same original question he had asked the petite brunette.

"An e-ecologist. I'd like to help p-protect our p-planet." The old man did not need to repeat the question as he pointed to the plump strawberry blonde seated behind the future ecologist.

"A lawyer," she said. The old man then pointed to student seated behind the plump blonde.

The dark-skinned young woman said aloud, "An artist and a philosopher."

"Engineer."

"Quarterback on a professional team, that or a plumber."

"Finances. Something in finances."

"Politician."

"Medical doctor."

"Cardiologist."

The old man rose from the desk chair deftly without showing signs of his apparent advanced age. He did not moan or grab his back in pain nor did he need to push off the desk to stand fully erect. He rose fluidly in a single motion as if he was the same age as the students. He walked towards the door, turned and glanced back at what he had written earlier on the blackboard. He stood in front of the freckled redhead who aspired to be a politician and remarked to the entire class, "Each of you harbor admirable career goals and aspirations. But with the possible exception of the artist-philosopher, all of you have chosen fields that have but trivial, fleeting moments of importance. At least the artist-philosopher has a chance, albeit a slim one, of creating something of value, perhaps a framework for malleable reasoning or a broader view of perception, or of our existence. While the rest of you will be cast into oblivion sooner than you realize or that you can now appreciate. The relevance of your existence, or should it please you, your importance to others you will encounter, will rapidly and definitively become nothing more than totally insignificant, and forever irrelevant."

The students were not able to speak with one voice but they all shared the same thought, as they did when they first laid eyes on the strange old man. Now, their singular thought was to defend their lives, their future and their very existence and since the entire class had nothing whatsoever to do with mathematics, as they were led to believe, they found themselves engaged in what they perceived to be an intellectual form of terrorism. It was time to retaliate.

The lanky blonde who dreamed of being a cardiologist was the first to go on the offensive. "Certainly, no one would think that my life as a healer, as someone who saves lives, would be considered insignificant. If on the operating table I use my skills, my talents, my learned ways to save the life of someone who then goes on to live a long and productive life, then no one could question the value of my existence."

"I agree," added the petite Asian who also aspires to be a medical doctor. "Those who heal others are extremely vital to our society. They keep us fit and healthy and free of diseases." The two close friends led the way for their classmates. After a brief moment of silence, everyone but the young lady with the beautiful brown skin and matching eyes who had declared her desire to be a philosopher and an artist spoke in turn. For the most part each mimicked what the first two said, namely that they would work to be important and to make a difference in people's lives. Declarations of worth grew bolder and bolder as their aspirations rose higher and higher. They ended with the declaration by the freckled-faced redhead seated in the first seat of row four that he was destined to climb the political ladder all the way to the office of the presidency of the United States of America.

The old man listened intently to each student's unrehearsed, and often impassioned speech. He showed little emotion other than the knitting of his eyebrows every now and again, and other than a step to his right and left, he stood firmly and unflinchingly in place as they spoke. He was in the classroom for a purpose and it was quite obvious to him that the purpose was well founded, and yet he was also intrigued by the inability of these students to appreciate what he was trying to convey. A more elevated, more personal and in many ways, a more obvious approach was necessary.

"By a show of hands, tell me how many of you know the name of either your mother, your father or your legal guardian?" All ten students raised their hands.

"Now how many of you know the name of the mother or father of that person?" Again, all ten hands shot up.

"Back further, how many of you know the name of the mother or father of that person, that is, the name of your great grandparents." This time only the hands of the Asian and the dark-skinned women rose.

"And would either of you know that name of your great, great grandparents?" The two women, seated at opposite ends of the room lowered their hands and shook their heads to signal no.

"Yes or no," the old man said as he strode towards the middle of the front of the room and leaned back on the teacher's wooden desk. "Was the existence of your great, great, grandparent important to you and to your existence?" Everyone in the class nodded in the affirmative.

"Important, and yet forgotten." The old man sighed heavily. "An operational definition of a generation is 25 years – from birth to the age of reproduction. So, counting yourself as the index generation none of you even know the name of the person who lived only four generations ago. Someone who you acknowledged to be vital to your existence; someone who lived perhaps oh, say 100 or so years ago, who had a job, a life, an existence and most likely a strongly held belief that they too were important and relevant to their extant family, to their successors, to the individual, to their neighbors and neighborhood, and to the whole of society, is a person who you cannot even name. There is a high probability that you have never even seen a photograph of these people despite the fact that photography was commonplace during their lifetime and I am willing to bet that none of you have even read a note or a letter written by them. They exist in the abstract, 'My great, great, grandfather worked at a shoe factory in the city' or 'My mother's, mother's mother came here from Europe when she was only 10 years old' and so on. These were real people who today, this very moment, are beyond dead. They are dead, decayed, decomposed and worse of all forgotten, and therefore they are now as they were always – irrelevant. And they differ from you only in one small way – you are alive and irrelevant. Your existence means nothing now and it will mean even less in the future. Your descendants, should you have any, will dismiss your existence just as easily as you dismissed that of your ancestors." The old man had more to say but he heard the tortured first letters from the curly haired stutterer.

"Y-you make it s-sound...sh-should we j-just k-k-kill ourselves now?"

"Do you want all of us to call it quits, throw in the towel? Is that what you want? I mean that's the point? Right? We have modern technology, advanced recording systems and advanced medical technology and other things that will keep us healthy and our memories alive for centuries to come," said the athlete who tried to weave too many ideas into one long-winded assault as if he was trying to call a simple run play using a string of 15 verbal codes.

"Centuries? How many centuries," the old man asked cuttingly. The athlete stabbed at a number without a thought.

"Five."

"Five centuries. Do I hear six?" the old man asked mockingly. "Or how about ten? Does ten centuries sound like a long time?

Will you be remembered 1,000 years from now? Anyone? No you will not. Can anyone name anyone who lived 1,000 years ago? Can anyone even tell me about a major world that occurred 1,000 years ago? Perhaps a cosmic event, anything?" Although some famous individuals – inventors, politicians, sports stars, ancient thinkers and even religious personas – from the past came to the mind of some students, no one answered. Exact dates and time periods eluded them. Subsequently, the room was again silent. But the old man wasn't done nor did he prod them for a name, he simply continued on.

"One year is one-thousandth of 1,000 years. Tell me, what did you do exactly a month ago that didn't involve school?"

The athlete felt as though he was being squeezed for an answer despite the fact that the old man was not looking in his direction. And with his signature flippant attitude replied loudly so that the whole class would hear him clearly, "I was snowboarding." The old man turned in his direction, took one look at him and instantly knew that the athlete was lying. It was not a matter of catching the student in the lie as much as it was determining how great the false statement would be expanded.

"Snowboarding. Tell us son, where did you snowboard?" Although the athlete was taken by surprise by the follow-up questions he nevertheless answered them with little hesitation.

"Yes, snowboarded. At a resort not far from here called MountainView. Great place," he lied outright because he assumed that the old man would know nothing of the relatively new winter sport or of the local mountains. The old man clasped his hands behind his back and began to pace in front of the classroom like a courtroom prosecutor who was about to cross-examine a witness.

"Did you go snowboarding on MountainView on a Saturday or on a Sunday? Was it sunny or cloudy or snowy? Was it a relatively warm day or was it a cold day?"

"It was a Sunday and it was cold, and it was snowing very hard, it was almost a blizzard."

The old man nodded.

"There is an unwritten expectation that humans communicate not only accurately but also honestly. If future generations are to understand who their ancestors were, what they accomplished, how they lived, then they must be certain that the storyteller does not spin fiction when fact was available. Every Sunday over the past six weeks were sunny and snowless; no one has snowboarded or skied on MountainView since it closed last year. You were neither near that mountain nor any other mountain on any of the past six Sundays. You were within a 5-mile radius of your house, likely at the gym. Young man, false statements serve only those who seek to profit from them. Are you trying to benefit from your deception?"

That the athlete did not repudiate the old man's claims caused the other students to silently gasp at what had transpired. First, one of their peers was caught in a flagrant lie and second, and far more importantly, the athlete also did not reject the old man's descriptions of his movements during the past month and a half worth of Sundays. How did the old man know what the athlete had done? Was it a wild guess? Did he know someone who knew the athlete?

It was at this point when the class shared another collective thought: Could there be more than meets the eye to this old man? But they didn't have long to think about the stranger's oddities before he volleyed the next question to the class.

"How long has your species, *Homo sapiens*, been in existence?"

Although they all listened intently, not one student replied. That the old man seemed to have excluded himself from belonging to the species escaped no one as now the class was on heightened alert for additional suspicious lines and phrases.

"*Two hundred thousand* years," the old man told the students. "And there's barely a trace of anyone or anything from those early days not to mention from those that lived five-thousand, two-thousand or even a thousand years ago. No. None of you, or anything associated with you, will exist 200 years from now. Thankfully, once your entire pathetic species self-destructs, nature will restore the entire planet to its pristine, aboriginal state in only 30,000 years or so, a cosmic blink of an eye."

Again, it was curly haired stammerer who aspired to be an ecologist that asked the old man essentially the same question he had asked a moment ago, "S-should we a-a-abandon all hope and not g-go t-through with our dreams?"

"Why do you insist on asking this question?" asked the old man somewhat irritated. "Why of course you should go on with your lives. But realize that your particular role, your impact – whether as a physician, a lawyer, an ecologist, a plumber or any other profession – will have no long-term relevance. Yes. By all means, have fun, reproduce, make money, help others or kill, if you must, but realize that the ramifications of your actions are of no lasting importance. Consider your lifespan. Now consider that number alongside the fact that it took 400,000 years for light to escape the chaos of the Big Bang, as you call it. Every photon of light that you perceive originated from that singular event; your own speck of faint light is meaningless. On a cosmic scale, your existence registers orders of magnitude below inconsequential. I cannot say it more simply, or more succinctly."

The old man then walked briskly walked towards the door from whence he entered as if suddenly realizing that he was late for an appointment. With his right hand on the doorknob he stopped, turned to the class and uttered his final words.

"Now most of you probably consider me to be irrelevant. And I agree with you completely. I have been and will always be totally unnecessary and quite useless. You see me as an old man, but it is only due to your present day perception. I am more than you'll ever know. Oh, one last thing. Should you choose to maintain some semblance of relevance, embrace those around you, and never leave this room." Then in a flash, the old man in a white button-down shirt, a brown pattern-less tie, a dark-gray vest and a well-worn brown herringbone tweed sports coat, brown trousers and worn dark brown leather shoes exited the room. The door closed behind him with conviction. Mounted high above the doorframe the sweep hand of the plain black clock with was still jerking from dash to dash to dash.

"Look," exclaimed the petite brunette who yearned to be a veterinarian. "It's not even eight o'clock."

∽

THROUGHOUT THEIR YOUNG LIVES, from the first frightening days at daycare to those short preschool sessions straight through to elementary school, middle school, and now high school, no adult or teacher had ever left them alone, unattended, in a room. There was no bell to signal the end of the class; no one to tell them that class was over, no one's voice over the speaker to indicate that the next period would start in seven minutes, nothing. They all sat utterly befuddled for a full moment until the athlete stood to stretch his arms and legs that had been packaged tightly in the one-piece desk. His movement caused the rest of the class to focus their attention inwards and, as such, they shifted their desks so that now they were, more or less, facing each other. Without a signal that gave them permission to disperse, the students did what came naturally to gatherings before the advent of modern electronics – they began to speak directly to each another.

"N-now i-it's eight-oh-one," declared the young man who had been fixated on the clock ever since the petite brunette who loved pets noticed that time had essentially stood still while the old man was in the room. "D-do y-y-you th-think the clock is right?"

"No joke. It's right! According to my watch, it's 8:01," replied the baby-faced young man who wanted to be an engineer. "Doesn't it seem like that man was in here for about an hour or so?" No one responded to this odd question for it was quite obvious that the old man was in the room for more than just a few seconds. Whether time stood still, or if something else could explain the time difference, was so perplexing that it was easier to simply ignore it then to try to understand it.

"No matter how long he was here, the old man obviously wasn't going to teach us mathematics. So, what gives? What was that all about?" asked the dark-skinned young lady who liked finances.

"Right? And has anyone seen him before or does anyone know why this room is like this? No windows? Old fashioned design? Blackboard? Has anyone been in here before? I thought all of the rooms in this wing were new," said the freckled-faced future politician. "It's kind of creepy."

"The room is interesting, but the bigger question is who was that man and why did he go out of his way to deliver such a depressing message?" asked the dark-skinned young lady who liked finances.

"I've never seen him before today, but he looked familiar. It's like I already knew him or I've run into him somewhere before, but I just don't know where," said the future artist and philosopher.

"True. He was like one of those people you see in those old family portraits, you know those formal pose pictures where most of the people were sitting and some were standing," added the smart young lady who sat in front of the future artist. "When you look at those people in those old photos and you really study their faces, their expression, their body language, you see someone you already know, like someone who is living today, here and now. One time I looked at one of these old pictures and I swear I saw myself standing there, like I was actually living at that time, in that place with those other people in that picture. In some ways, that old man gave me those same strange feelings. I was intrigued by his presence more than his message."

"Th-that's g-good because his message was p-p-pointless. How c-could anyone th-th-think w-w-we're not important, meaningful, or re-re-reverent?" asked the curly hair stutterer.

"Relevant," said the future cardiologist from diagonally across the room. "You mean 'relevant', not 'reverent'. And the old man was saying that we, all of us, become irrelevant, non-important and totally forgotten quicker than we think. He asked us good questions about our not-so-distant relatives that supported his stance, and I have to admit, I think he's right."

"I agree. When you think about it, there is not much that we can do, or should I say that there has been little that others before us have done, that has had lasting qualities," added the cardiologist's friend who was seated in front of her. "As I think about it there is no one in my family that has done anything of durable importance. Even old letters and diaries we found in my grandmother's attic when I was a kid were interesting but only for a moment. We skimmed them, and then we threw them away because no one wanted to be bothered with them. None of us saw the value of storing them any longer; in preserving our past. They just took up space. And now everything we type or text is even less permanent."

Everyone in the class commented and over the next few minutes, one opinion was quickly followed another.

"But at one time someone treasured those things, right? Or else why would anyone have kept them in the first place? They must have had some kind of value."

"I suppose if you're sentimental, then keepsakes like diaries and letters would have some value."

"But for how long?"

"Right. That's what the old man said. Even if the sentimentality trait was handed down to three generations, it still wouldn't add up to much time. It just goes to show you that our view of time is narrow, extremely narrow. There's no two ways about that."

"So, we're irrelevant. Now what? Do we just quit? Call it a day? End this life now or live it out to the max?"

"Right. I mean there have been, what hundreds of billions of people that have lived on this planet? And most all of them would easily qualify as having had no measurable or lasting impact on this planet or on our society..."

"... for better or for worse, right?"

"And game over when you extend these concepts beyond our little sandbox."

"Exactly. Every speck of life that ever vibrated, crawled, wiggled, swam, flew or walked on this planet, every speck combined, did not alter the greater universe one stinking iota."

It was the freckled faced redhead that longed to be a politician who sat in the first seat of the fourth row, the desk nearest the door where the old man both entered and exited, who said in his still youthful, higher-than-expected pitched voice, the last sentence that ended with, "...one stinking iota," a statement so convincing that it caused the class to end that part of the conversation.

The students were in their own thoughts for the next few minutes, each digesting the ramifications and weight of their own irrelevance. Even the athlete who always thought he had a place in the world because of his superb coordination, as well as the future artist-philosopher, who was granted an encouraging nod from the old man, now questioned their worth. It seemed as though the longer the silence lingered, the longer it would continue. It was, after all, a heavy moment of realization for the ten young students; such defining moments were typically reserved for adults, not them. They woke that morning without such heaviness. They were just ten high school students slogging through another first day of class as they had done so many times before having suffered no more than a paper cut. But today they found themselves not only teacher-less but also feeling depressed and quite worthless, as if the sure winds that had always filled their idealistic sails suddenly, and quite unexpectedly, stilled.

It was the bold brunette who would one day become a veterinarian who broke the long silence with a thought that snapped her classmates out of their stupor. "What," she started, "what if that old man was crazy? I mean I've never seen him before. Perhaps he was a lunatic that stumbled into our building from the streets and into the room to just spout some 'end of the world' craziness?"

"H-he didn't sound cr-cr-crazy to me."

"Nor I. He was odd, all right but I don't think he had dementia or anything. I just think he came in here to relay a message and well, I guess we all heard that message loud and clear."

"Does anyone think that there is a connection between the old man and the layout of this room, with the chalkboard, and old maps and everything?"

"Maybe."

"Could it be that the décor of this room is one of those intentional things designed to strengthen the message of the lesson?"

"You mean like we think it's old fashion, when it really was in style not that long ago?"

"Exactly."

"I think you're right. I missed it altogether. But now that you pointed it out, it's true. Our lives are so transient, so brief, so insignificant that we don't even realize it even when it's right under our nose. It's scary, really."

"Not to mention that most of us are seniors. For the first time in our lives we are young seniors. In just a few more decades, we'll be old seniors. Imagine that?"

∼

Discomfort in the small, one-piece desk again caused the athlete to spring out of his seat to stretch his muscular frame. His sudden movement caused the others to contemplate rising from their desks as well but since there was no audible signal nor an adult voice that demanded such behavior the most anyone else did was to shift slightly in their seats and watch the future plumber and hopeful NFL player reach for the ceiling with arms and fingers outstretched.

"I'm leaving," the athlete declared half-heartedly.

"What? You're going to just leave?" asked the dark-skinned young lady that sat directly behind the athlete in a voice that transmitted both shock with fear. "Just like that with no permission or bell or anything?"

"And what about the old man's warning about leaving the room?" continued the engineer-type who looked equally astonished. "We have a chance at being relevant if we stay together and I for one don't want to leave. Please don't leave."

"Whatever we do we should do it together," opined the plump strawberry blonde. "We should stay or we should go as one. There is strength in numbers and together we have a chance of surviving this ordeal, whatever this ordeal is."

"Right! What ordeal?" questioned the athlete who instinctively wanted to run but remained firmly in place. "We're not captives, are we? We have to leave sometime, right?"

"But if the old man is right, then we need to stay together or else...." The future politician's line of thought failed him. He wasn't sure what was up or what was down, if the time had stopped or moved along without them, or if the decision that needed to be made would be the right one. Indeed, his inability to formulate clear solutions would serve him well in his inevitable career as a representative, then eventually as a senator.

"Or the meaning of the old man's message could be lost," said the petite Asian. "Clearly," she continued, "he was telling us that we needed to live in the moment, to embrace what we have here and now, treasure those around us because life, like time, is fleeting. The future is not important because it may not happen and the past is worthless because memories become meaningless. So, we need to enjoy our relevance right now for tomorrow, or perhaps even later today, it may dissipate. Our relevance may be gone."

As before, the class, that is everyone but the athlete who was already standing, sat stoically. After a solid five minutes, they decided to leave the room together, in unison in an effort to maintain their relevance among themselves. Five of the students moved towards the door under the black clock while the other five moved towards the door located to the back of the room. They waited until each small group had gathered tightly at each exit, and in synchrony, the two individuals – one at each door – slowly turned the knob and opened it.

What the students saw shocked them to their core.

The hallway was in ruins. It was not clean and shiny but rather it was decayed and old with broken linoleum floor and crumbly red bricks walls, dusty mortar with fluorescent lights and fixtures with wires dangling from the broken ceiling; a hallway was dangerously impassable.

Shaken, the ten students turn back into the room and sat in

the exact small one-piece desks they had vacated just a moment ago.

All ten students had the same thought: *Is this some kind of joke?*

∽

THE EMPTY-HANDED OLD man spotted a bronze marker embedded just ahead in the cracked asphalt pavement. Apparently, some high school class leaders of long ago not only thought that future generations would be interested in the once-meaningful items deposited in the time capsule but also that the timepiece itself would not be forsaken. He shook his head and smiled wryly as he continued to walk across the dusty, weed and debris-strewn lot that contained the long ago condemned high school building.

Inside the abandoned post-WWII era structure, were ten indecisive young adults seated in a classroom mulling their relevance, as were countless other groups of children, and adults scattered throughout the same worn building, and in many other like buildings peppered about the planet. Down the once vibrant street lined with perfectly aligned, triple-decker homes strolled the old man. He walked neither briskly nor slowly for what may have been hours until he reached the outskirt of the old sector. A few of the more curious among those within eyeshot turned and looked in his direction, but most were indifferent to the old man, to his black, Browline wayfarer glasses and to his odd style of clothing. With caution, but with ease, the old man stepped onto the long hovercraft that then quietly glided away from the station as it has done punctually at this exact time, 8:00 a.m., for tens of decades.

∽

THE MOTION DETECTORS WORKED FLAWLESSLY.

As soon as Mr. Mann entered room K78, the lights not only turned on but they also adjusted appropriately to mix with the ambient light that streamed through the energy producing windows; a condition that provided the correct wavelength and the right amount of light needed to create an optimal learning environment.

In synchrony, all ten students were jolted awake.

It seemed to the empty-handed Mr. Mann as though each student had his or her head atop on their left or right forearm sound asleep at exactly 8:00 a.m. when he entered the dim room. Mr. Mann and the still seated students momentarily shared a moment of the reciprocated shock; neither the individual nor the collective group was prepared for the appearance of the other.

"Is this some kind of a joke?" asked the affable math instructor. "Or was everyone up late last night reviewing the final exam from last semester's pre-calculus course?"

"What the hell?" asked Brian, the athlete, in a slow, deliberate voice as he looked at his desk, then panned the room as if he had never before sat at a comfortable desk or seen the inside of a modern classroom. "Hey Wayne, mister engineer, tell me what the hell is going on here," Brian said to his classmate with thick glasses seated to his left. Wayne's slacked-jawed look of bewilderment only subtracted time from his childish face to the point that he didn't even seem old enough to be in high school, let alone in a course on advanced mathematics.

Mr. Mann, arms folded, leaned back against the huge multi-purpose whiteboard and tried to make sense of the situation. He has seen quite a bit over his 35 years of teaching math at Cathedral Ledge High School, but he never walked into a classroom, on the first day of class or on any other day for that matter, to find students asleep at their desks. This was not even April's

Fools day, when harmless practical jokes were commonplace. As Mr. Mann watched Cathy, the last of the ten students to stir awake, he became convinced that this was not a classroom of aspiring actors following a well-rehearsed script. Rather, he thought, the odds were high that the classroom's climate control system temporarily malfunctioned and that, somehow, the entire class was exposed to something, such as carbon monoxide, that caused their weariness. There was no other logical explanation.

"Donald. Can you tell me what is going on here?" the teacher asked the curly-haired future ecologist who sat in the first desk in the first row.

"I-I-I have n-n-no idea wh-wh-whatsoever, Mister Mann. Something is f-f-funny." Taking advantage of the math teacher's sightline, Sheryl, the future lawyer who sat directly behind Donald, tried to describe to Mr. Mann what had transpired before his arrival.

"Mister Mann," Sheryl began in a sure voice not unlike that of a seasoned prosecutor, "just moments ago, while we were waiting for you to arrive, an old man entered the classroom, but not exactly this classroom, but rather one from a bygone era. It was like a classroom out of my grandparent's day or maybe even earlier, I'm not sure. This old man had an odd philosophical message. He told us, in no uncertain terms, that we were unnecessary."

"Irrelevant," chimed in Kim, the dark-skinned philosopher seated directly behind Sheryl.

"Right, that's the word he used repeatedly, 'irrelevant'. He said that we, all of us, our ways, our lives, our entire being was irrelevant," said Sheryl continuing where she had left off.

Mr. Mann listened patiently with arms still folded. He then turned to his left to look at Leanne, the aspiring heart surgeon, as she added, "In context to cosmic time and space, the old man explained that we are overly fixated with the big picture of our existence, which is not that meaningful relative to the present moment which is highly relevant. Our perceived importance to current society or to our legacy is inconsequential – the moment is everything." Petite Mary, Leanne's good friend nodded in agreement whereas George, who would one day preside over the State's senate, was clearly agitated.

"Mister Mann, something very unusual happened here this morning. I really could care less about the old man's philosophy or whatever he was trying to say, as much as I am with the entire scene. After we had this back and forth bantering about our place in the universe, the crazy old man suddenly left the room and he told us that if we wanted to remain relevant then we should embrace each other and not leave this room; not this room of course, but the old fashion room that this room was like when we arrived. So he leaves and we discuss the situation for some time then we decide to leave but when we opened the door, well the door led to a destroyed hallway. We couldn't have left if we wanted to."

"The old man did say that math was relevant," added Christine, the dark skinned young lady who would eventually become the vice president of the local bank. "So I wouldn't say that he was completely crazy, just a bit odd."

The behavior of this class, these ten students, was uncharted territory for the veteran math instructor. Over his long teaching career, he dealt with unruly students, idle threats on his life, sit-in protests to his rigid grading practices, and outright disrespect. Also, there were the parents of disgruntled students who only served to demonstrate to Mr. Mann the power of genetics. More than once he wondered how genes for poor reasoning and low intellect were able to survive to present day only to conclude that if they were carried along for this long, then they were probably irreversibly linked to genes for an involuntary trait, such as blinking.

"What I am hearing is that when you arrived in this classroom this morning, it really wasn't like it is now, but instead it was an old style classroom and in my place was an old man who spoke mainly of your place in the greater universe that amounted to no more than zero on a cosmic scale. Then, after the mystery man left, you also decide to leave the room but the hallway was impassible, as if you were in some sort of a condemned building. Then I show up and startle you out of a nap. Is that correct?"

"E-e-exactly," stammered Donald who seemed to hang on every word as if he was waiting for Mr. Mann to say something that needed to be corrected. Although the high school enrolled over 1,500 students, Mr. Mann knew some of the students in this class, namely Leanne, Mary, and Wayne, from having previously taught them Geometry. They were serious students who did not seem to be the sort to participate in a scheme to deceive him. Mr. Mann looked at Wayne, Mary and Leanne and all three familiar students were nodding to affirm Donald's statement.

With less than 35 minutes left in the hour-long class, Mr. Mann had nothing else to do but to activate a hidden projector with a tiny handheld controller. The whiteboard at the front of the room projected the day's lesson that amounted to no more than a review of the key elements of pre-calculus. The ten students, whose minds were still grappling with the day's events, did their best to follow Mr. Mann's accelerated teaching pace.

For a few moments over the next half-hour, life returned to normal.

The familiar teacher taught, the high-energy projector projected, the numbers appeared on the whiteboard and the students seated in modern classroom were absorbed in the lesson. Everything about the scholastic scene was relevant, necessary and outright meaningful.

The soft tone that seemed to be emitted by the digital clock above the door indicated that it was exactly 9:00 a.m. It signaled the end of the first period of the day. The students knew that they had ten minutes to get themselves to the next class yet no one moved. Not one soul.

Mr. Mann looked at the class in amazement. "Are you not leaving?"

"After you," suggested George who sat closest to the door to the front of the classroom.

"That's fine by me," replied Mr. Mann who turned off the high-energy projector with a click of the little controller. He then stooped to reach underneath the modern desk, straightened up and turned to his left towards the door in the front of the classroom. No fewer than twenty eyes watched Mr. Mann leave room K78 firmly clutching, in his right hand, a tan leather briefcase.

THE LIGHTS slowly dimmed until they finally turned off, leaving room K78 pitch black. The motion detectors that activated the lights worked flawlessly.

## THE END

ACKNOWLEDGEMENT

The author is grateful to Bonnie Lawrence for providing critical review, suggestions and commentary.

ABOUT THE AUTHOR

L.C. Paoletti is a microbiologist and an aspiring writer. He is the author of *The Last Hypothesis*, and *Abby's Theory*, and an ebook titled *EOL2Die4*. This is his first book of short stories.